C

The Silver Box

Other Scholastic titles by the same author:

Two Parents Too Many

Curse of The Silver Box

BRENDA BELLINGHAM

Cover by
Ernie Cselko and Susan Gardos

Scholastic-TAB Publications Ltd.

Scholastic-TAB Publications Ltd.
123 Newkirk Road, Richmond Hill, Ontario, Canada L4C 3G5

Scholastic Inc.
730 Broadway, New York, NY 10003, USA

Ashton Scholastic Limited
165 Marua Road, Panmure, PO Box 12328, Auckland 6, New
Zealand

Ashton Scholastic Pty Limited
PO Box 579, Gosford, NSW 2250, Australia

Scholastic Publications Ltd.
Holly Walk, Leamington Spa, Warwickshire CV32 4LS,
England

Canadian Cataloguing in Publication Data
Bellingham, Brenda, 1931-
    The curse of the silver box

ISBN 0-590-73296-X

I. Title.

PS8553.E468C87 1989   jC813'.54   C88-095302-0
PZ7.B45Cu 1989

9 8 7 6 5 4 3 2 1   Printed in Canada   0 1 2 3 4 5/9
Manufactured by Webcom Limited

Contents

1. Don' t Say I Didn't Warn You 1

2. It's a Mystery 10

3. The Hayley-Smiths 16

4. The Black Spot 25

5. Cursed 33

6. The Burglary 41

7. An Accident 48

8. Liar! 58

9. Wild Goose Chase 66

10. Dad in Danger 76

11. Running Out of Time 87

12. A Hunch 94

13. Unhappy Kid 104

14. The Rightful Owner 109

15. How it Ended 121

Chapter 1

Don't Say I Didn't Warn You

Last Halloween, I went to an auction sale. Big mistake! But when you're thirteen years old the trick-or-treat routine seems a bit childish. So I went to the sale with my dad and my stepmother, Vivian.

Something was different about this auction. I knew it right away. The warehouse it was being held in was kind of spooky. There were so many rooms of all sizes and shapes leading off one another that walking around them was like trying to find your way through a maze. In spite of the fans high up in the rafters, there was a fusty smell from the items waiting to be sold — old things, bits of other people's lives, discarded things. Sad, maybe. Definitely mysterious — like watchful ghosts.

Then Vivian called out to me. She was standing at the door of a tiny room I hadn't noticed before.

"Katy, come and look at this."

I edged my way to her through the collection of precious antiques. Vivian held out a small silver box engraved with figures. "Isn't it marvellous?" she said.

I'd never seen anything like it before. The box was so old that the engravings had worn away in places and you had to look closely to make out the figures. A smiling cat lay in the centre, surrounded by angels and saints. At least, Vivian and I decided they must be angels and saints. They were all wearing long gowns, and some had wings.

"You don't usually see a cat associated with religious figures," Vivian said, thoughtfully. "This box must be incredibly old. Medieval, probably."

That's when I looked up from the box and saw this creepy kid staring at Vivian. He was only about nine years old, with black hair and blue eyes. He would've been good-looking if he hadn't had such a mean expression and such intense, hard eyes. I couldn't help looking into his eyes, even though I didn't want to.

He scared me. Not that I expected him to pull a knife, or a pair of knuckle dusters. Actually he was kind of a scrawny little kid. He was wearing designer jeans and a black leather jacket which looked new. It also looked too big for him, which didn't help the tough image. But he still gave me the creeps. Those eyes were really spooky.

Vivian turned the box upside down. "I wonder what these tiny marks mean. I don't think they're craftsman's marks." She turned it right side up and looked at the cat again. "This cat reminds me of Sam," she said, smiling. "Look at its smug expression."

There was something Sam-like about it. Even though I didn't see quite as much of our cat as I used to, I'd have recognized that self-satisfied smirk anywhere.

Sam lives with my dad and Vivian now. After Mother and Dad got divorced, Mother got custody of me, my sister, Jenny, and Sam. Then Mother decided she wanted to marry her boyfriend, Adam. Adam's allergic to cat fur, so Dad and Vivian took Sam to live with them. Mother and Adam kept Jenny and me. We still see quite a lot of Sam, because ours is not your usual divorced family. Our two sets of parents work hard at getting along.

"What's the box for?" I asked.

Vivian knows a lot about antiques. She and Dad own an antique shop in the Yorkville district of Toronto.

"I'm not sure." She hesitated. "If it really is medieval, it might have been a reliquary."

"Whatever that is," I said.

I knew Vivian would set me straight. She thinks I might go into the antique business when

I'm older, so she tries to teach me about it. Also, it's something she gets to do with me that Mother doesn't. Mother hates antiques.

"In medieval times people collected hair, or nail parings, or other body parts, or bits of clothing that were supposed to have come from saints," Vivian went on. "They called them relics. Such things were believed to be very holy. People kept them in boxes like this, which they called reliquaries."

"Gross," I said.

But in spite of what it might have been used for, the box itself was gorgeous. It even felt gorgeous — smooth and silky, as though countless generations of people had held it.

"Why don't you buy it?" I asked Vivian. I could see she really wanted it. She was just about drooling over it.

Looking back, I sure wish I'd kept my mouth shut!

"I don't think your father and I can afford it," Vivian said.

Dad was lost somewhere among the four-poster beds, wardrobes, china cabinets and high-backed dining chairs, but eventually he found his way out of the furniture forest and joined us. Vivian, her eyes shining, showed him the box.

"You can't kid me," he said, smiling at her with eyes full of love. "You don't want to buy that expensive little item for the shop, you want it for yourself, don't you?" He put his arm around her.

Watching Dad and Vivian together made me feel like a stranger visiting someone else's family. I didn't feel jealous of Vivian. (In fact, I'm probably the only thirteen-year-old in the world who really likes her stepmother.) But sometimes, I felt as if she and Dad lived in a private world that didn't include me. I looked away.

"Go ahead and bid on it," Dad said.

I didn't hear what Vivian answered, because I was looking straight into the glittering eyes of the creepy kid.

He was standing with his feet planted firmly apart and staring, really staring, at Vivian. Hadn't he ever seen a pregnant woman before?

Vivian's tall and willowy, but because she was seven months pregnant with her first baby, she was a willow with a knobby trunk. She still looked classy, though. In fact, she kind of shone, like those crystal drops you hang in your window to catch the light. She certainly didn't deserve to be stared at the way that kid was staring.

Even though he made me nervous, I glared at him to let him know what I thought of his manners. It didn't faze him.

Vivian put the box back on the shelf where it belonged. Deep in discussion, she and Dad wandered away. As soon as they'd gone, the kid grabbed the box. One of the attendants came and put his hand on the boy's shoulder.

"Young man," he said, "I must warn you that if you break anything your parents will have to pay for it." He spoke softly, but I was close enough to overhear.

The kid smiled in a sneering way. In a clear, confident voice, he announced, "I'm not going to break anything. You are."

I couldn't quite believe what he did next. It was too bizarre. He held the relic box at chest level, between his palms. As he gazed coldly at the attendant, I could hear him muttering something. The man's thin nose turned white. The boy seemed to make him nervous too.

Who does he think he's kidding? I thought. Is he trying to cast a spell or something? I figured he'd rather be out collecting candies and this was his idea of a Halloween trick.

But then the attendant moved away and picked up a china vase that the boy had left near the edge of a table. When he set it down on a higher shelf, his sleeve somehow caught it. The vase toppled to the floor, shattering into a thousand pieces. "Oh!" The man gave a cry of despair.

"What did I tell you?" asked the boy, smiling.

Creepy kid!

A girl a couple of years older than I am, about the same age as my sister Jenny, came and tore the box out of the boy's hands. She put it back where it belonged, and dragged the kid away. I followed Dad and Vivian.

"There you are, Katy," said Dad. "Come along, the auction's about to start." He steered Vivian and me to the seats in front of the auctioneer's stand.

Out of the corner of my eye, I saw the girl and the creepy kid sitting about two rows in front of us. I figured the girl must be the weirdo's older sister. She had pale blonde hair, straight with bangs. It swung close to her face, like a curtain she wanted to hide behind. She caught me looking, blushed, and quickly looked away.

"Ahem. Ahem." The man who was with them cleared his throat to attract their attention.

He had dark hair like the brat, but his was so black you'd think he'd been using boot polish for hair cream. He wore tinted glasses, the kind that let you see other people but don't let other people see you, and he kept his overcoat collar turned up. I admit it was just about November, but it wasn't that cold. It figured that the weird kid would have an equally weird father!

"Number one," said the auctioneer. "A seventeenth century pine . . ."

I didn't pay much attention to the auction. My mind was on other things. Until then, Vivian's baby had never seemed quite real to me. I'd thought of it as kind of doll-soft and cuddly and smelling of baby powder. But watching the boy and his sister had made me think about what would happen when the baby grew up a bit. Suddenly I realized that it wouldn't always be a baby. With my luck it'd grow into a brat, like the one two rows in front. Dad would spoil it. He'd be as crazy over the kid as he was over Vivian.

"Number 51."

Dad nudged me. Number 51 was the box. I felt a tingle of excitement. "Don't blink, Katy," Dad whispered, grinning, "they might think you're making a bid."

He wasn't kidding. This wasn't one of those auctions where the auctioneer sings out cheerfully. Everything was quiet. It was hard to tell who was bidding.

In front of us, the father of the brat raised one finger. The auctioneer said, "Thank you, sir." The boy and his sister sat on the edge of their chairs, breathing heavily.

I knew how they felt. The longer the bidding went on, the more I wanted Vivian to have that silver box. My heart pounded. You'd have thought I was running a race.

Finally, the bidding slowed down. The father dropped out. The family went into a huddle. I could tell the kids were trying to persuade their dad to bid some more. Finally, he sprang up from his seat. He looked as if he couldn't take any more.

While I was watching all this, I missed the most exciting part. Vivian won. The relic box with the smiling cat on it was hers.

"Well done," Dad said.

The brat's father mopped his forehead with a large, white handkerchief as he marched towards the exit. The girl scuttled after him with her head down. She didn't see her little brother dart down the empty row behind us.

He leaned over Vivian's shoulder and hissed, "That's my box. Mine." He shot out his hand and dropped something into her lap. Then his father grabbed him and frog-marched him out.

Vivian sat there, stunned.

"What's this?" Dad whispered. "A love letter? Some young swain trying to steal my wife?"

That brought Vivian back to her senses. She smiled, picked up the paper, unfolded it, and held it so that Dad and I could read it too. Printed in pencil were the words:

"Look at the runes on the bottom of the box. This is what they say —"

The next part was written in ink in beautiful, slanting writing, but what the writing said wasn't beautiful:

"Cursed be ye who keep this box from its rightful owner. Thee and thine shall suffer and perish."

And, underneath, printed in pencil:

"Don't say I didn't warn you."

Chapter 2

It's a Mystery

Vivian gasped and dropped the paper. I picked it up so that I could read it again.

"How horrible," she whispered. Her cheeks and neck were scarlet.

Dad's face turned brick red. He jumped up. "Let me get my hands on that kid —" he began. He glared around the room, but the boy and his family were long gone.

Dad recovered his dignity, straightened his tie and buttoned his jacket. He put his hand under Vivian's elbow.

"Don't let it upset you, Vivian," he said. "Come along. We'll pay for the box and go home."

I put the piece of paper in my jeans pocket. Vivian's face had turned from scarlet to white and I figured she'd rather not see the note again.

I thought it was kind of neat, myself. It was

a big improvement over "If this book should chance to roam, Box its ears and send it home." Jenny and I used to write that in every book we owned.

When I got home, Jenny was sitting in front of her dressing table mirror, scowling at herself.

Jenny is fifteen, so she spends a lot of time in front of mirrors. She has shoulder length blonde hair and she's always moaning that it's too fine to style. She says it isn't fair that I inherited thick, dark hair from Mother, while she got hair like Dad's.

But when I told her about the box and its curse, her scowl disappeared, she gave up trying to make her hair stand on end, and she turned to me with a delighted grin.

"You mean Vivian freaked out when she read the kid's message?" she asked. "I don't believe it! She acts so sophisticated. Seems she's not so cool after all."

"Listen," I said, "that message was scary. That kid was scary. You're always down on Vivian. Face it, Jenny, you hardly know her."

Neither did I. I only thought I did. People are very hard to know. They're like icebergs. Only the tip shows. Most of them is below the water line where you can't see what's going on. Sometimes, as I found out later, there are even parts of yourself that can surprise you.

After I'd told Jenny, and my friend, DeeDee, who loves anything ghoulish, about the curse, I put it out of my mind. I had other things to think about.

For as long as I can remember, my dearest ambition has been to be a ballet dancer. I work hard and my teachers tell me I have talent.

In the new year, the school where I take my classes was putting on a public performance. The director, Miss Lightfoot, (honestly, that's her name) was retiring and the performance was in her honour. Some famous people in the ballet world were invited, so it was an important event for a would-be ballerina like me. The auditions for parts were coming up and I was hoping to be picked for one of the solos. That was all I could think about.

Later in the week, I came home from ballet class to find Mother gone. Jenny was in the basement practicing the piano. Our stepfather, Adam, sat on the chesterfield surrounded by a stack of term papers. Adam's a professor of zoology. He has a beard and he mostly wears baggy corduroys and old sweaters three times too big for him. He looks like a beat-up old teddybear. Jenny and I still didn't know him very well either. We'd only had him for a stepfather for about three months.

"Hi, Adam. Where's Mother?" I asked.

He looked up from the paper he was marking. "Hi, Katy," he said. "Vivian telephoned. She wasn't feeling well. Your father's away on business, so your mother went over."

As divorced families go, ours is pretty bizarre.

Mother came home quite late.

"What's wrong with Vivian?" I asked.

"Nothing much," Mother said. "She had a tummy-ache. She thought the baby might be coming, so she got a bit nervous." Mother has black hair and brown eyes. She's small and pretty, but very feisty. She reminds me of a boiled candy — hard on the outside, soft in the centre. Mostly she tries not to let anybody see her soft centre.

"So? Was it the baby?" Jenny asked impatiently. She had come upstairs when she heard Mother come home.

"No, of course not," Mother said.

Mother thinks that being sick is a sign of weakness in your character. It means you haven't been taking your vitamins and exercising regularly.

"As I told Vivian," she said, "there's quite a difference between a pain in the tummy and labour pains." She smiled in a superior way. She knew all about it because she'd had Jenny and me. "I advised her to see the doctor tomorrow."

So there was nothing to worry about, after all. But a few days later, we heard that Vivian's mother was in the hospital. She'd been planning to come from Nova Scotia to help with the new baby. When she heard that Vivian wasn't feeling well, she'd decided to come right away. But as she was leaving the house to go to the airport, she'd slipped on a patch of ice and fractured her arm.

The next day, when Dad phoned, I answered.

"Katy, my love, how would you and Jenny like to join me in a bit of detective work on Sunday afternoon?" he asked.

"Sounds like fun to me," I said. "What d'you want us to do?"

"Come with me to visit a Mrs. Hayley-Smith. It seems she's the previous owner of the little relic box with the cat on it."

"How d'you know?" I asked.

"Simple, my dear Watson," Dad said. "I asked the auctioneer."

"Some detective," I said. "So why d'you want to visit this Mrs. Hayley-Smith?"

Dad hesitated, then he decided to take me into his confidence. "Katy, do you remember those marks inscribed on the base of the box? Well, I took the box to a university professor who specializes in old forms of writing. He confirmed that the marks really are runes. They actually say what the boy said they did. How would a child know that, unless the box had once belonged to him?"

I couldn't come up with a good answer. "Truly amazing," I said.

"Besides," Dad went on, trying to sound nonchalant, "Vivian's taken it into her head that the curse on the box is responsible for her not feeling well, and for her mother's accident. The doctor said it's not good for her to get upset, so I promised I'd try to find the boy's family."

Vivian must be pretty sick. What if she lost the baby! "Why don't you go straight to the boy's father?" I asked. "Doesn't the auctioneer know who he was?"

"Unfortunately, no," Dad said. "It seems the man gave the auctioneer a false name and address. That's why finding the boy is going to take a bit of detective work. The thing is, Katy, I don't want to sound as if I suspect Mrs. Hayley-Smith of some sort of crime. I thought if I took my two lovely daughters along it would appear more like a social call."

"You don't have to be sarcastic," I said. "Why don't you just phone her?"

"Because I want to be able to watch her face when I confront her," Dad said. "You know, the start of guilt, the flush of embarrassment, that sort of thing. Katy, if you still have the piece of paper that boy gave Vivian, bring it with you."

"You think Mrs. Hayley-Smith might have stolen the box from the boy and then sold it?" I asked.

"I honestly don't know what to think," Dad said. "Why would the boy's father go to an auction and bid on a valuable antique if it had been stolen from him? He'd be more likely to go to the police. It's a mystery. And, frankly, I'd like to get to the bottom of it."

Chapter 3

The Hayley-Smiths

"Count Jenny and me in," I said. "Unless Mother and Adam have already made big plans for Sunday."

That's one of the problems with having two sets of parents. If they both want to drag you somewhere on the same day you have to choose between them, and the pair you don't choose feels hurt. At supper I brought the matter up for discussion.

Mother looked disappointed. "Adam and I thought it would be nice if the four of us went cross-country skiing on Sunday," she said. "But if your father needs you I suppose we could go another time."

Mother bends over backwards to be what she calls "fair" in sharing us with Dad. She seems to have one of those pie diagrams in her head — the kind you see in textbooks. Mother's diagram is called "Jenny and Katy pie" and she cuts it into neat wedges. Each wedge stands for our various activities. She cuts the piece left over down the middle — one half for her and one for Dad. But if one piece comes out smaller than the other she takes it, because that's the polite thing to do. Like I said, our parents work at getting along.

On Sunday, Dad picked us up in the station wagon. Jenny and I both crowded into the front seat with him. I sat in the middle.

"Dad, tell us more about those creepy runes on the box Vivian bought," I said, as we waited for a green light. "I read about runes in *The Hobbit*, but I didn't know that people ever really used them."

"I don't think ordinary people ever did use them much," Dad said. "They were mainly religious or magical symbols. In Denmark they've been found written on ancient grave markers. A chief's belongings were buried with him — precious things — and the runes were used to scare away thieves."

"The power of words!" Jenny said.

"Unfortunately, in more modern times runes were adopted by evil people when they wanted to express their hate for others," Dad said.

"Like that boy and his curse," I said, getting into the spirit of things. "He's probably the devil in disguise."

Jenny gave me a pitying look. "Didn't anyone

ever tell you that the devil is a grown man with a tail and horns?"

"I said he was in disguise," I said.

"The devil wouldn't disguise himself as a little boy," Jenny said. "A child isn't powerful enough to do the devil's work."

"You didn't meet this kid," I said.

"I agree with Jenny," said Dad. "A little boy didn't make up that curse or write those runes. What I want to know is, who did?" He frowned. "In my opinion, people who dabble in black magic are a menace to humankind."

My imagination went into overdrive, and my skin came up in goosepimples. I remembered the boy's father, with his coal black hair, hiding behind his dark glasses, and the girl hiding behind her curtain of hair. What if the whole family practiced black magic?

I didn't altogether mind the shiver that ran up my spine. It was something like the thrill you get on rides at a carnival. We had left downtown Toronto and were in the Casa Loma area. Mrs. Hayley-Smith lived in a stone mansion behind a high stone wall, in what had once been a very high class district. Now, some of the houses had been turned into apartments or offices.

Dad rang the bell and we heard it jangling deep inside the house. A tiny lady dressed in a brown skirt, brown sweater and brown shoes opened the door.

"Mrs. Hayley-Smith?" Dad asked as he handed her his business card. "Good afternoon. I'm Robert Martin. I phoned for an appointment earlier in the week." Dad has perfect manners. The lady gave a sort of gasp. "Oh no, I'm Dora, Mrs. Hayley-Smith's housekeeper. Please come in. I'll take you through to the library." She spoke with an English accent.

Head down, she scurried across a wide foyer tiled in black and white. On the far side of the hall, she opened a heavy oak door for us. "Please go in," she said.

The room was lined with books on three sides, floor to ceiling and wall to wall. The fourth wall was covered with paintings. Highly polished desks and tables were scattered everywhere, covered with vases, lamps, sculptures and knick-knacks. The room looked like an antique shop. Dad's eyes lit up. Mrs. Hayley-Smith, a large, middle-aged lady, was sitting at one end of a chesterfield facing the door. She wore a cotton dress, patterned with flowers, and a wide-brimmed straw hat. She looked as if she'd just come in from gardening. She even had dirt under her nails. In November!

Standing stiffly behind her, like a butler, was a grey-haired man. All I could see was the top half of him over the back of the chesterfield. He had a very short, bristly mustache, as if he'd forgotten to shave, and he wore a plaid shirt, open at the neck. He wasn't the butler. He was Mrs. Hayley-Smith's husband, Major Hayley-Smith.

After Dad introduced us, Mrs. Hayley-Smith poured tea from a silver teapot. She patted the chesterfield for Dora and the major to sit beside her. Mrs. Hayley-Smith and the major were the sort of people who believe in spreading themselves around. Poor little Dora huddled between them, her arms drawn in and her hands clasped around her knees. Mrs. Hayley-Smith sounded English, too, but her accent wasn't the same as Dora's.

"Now, Mr. Martin," simpered Mrs. Hayley-Smith while she served us some tea. "You were very mysterious on the phone, I must say. We're simply dying of curiosity, aren't we?" She smiled coyly at the major and Dora.

Dora said nothing. She kept her head down and looked miserable. Major Hayley-Smith stared straight ahead, as if he wished we'd go away. From time to time he cleared his throat like a walrus warning people to keep off its territory.

Mrs. Hayley-Smith turned to Dad. "What can we do for you, Mr. Martin?"

Dad put down his cup. With a flourish, he took the box with its smiling cat out of its packing and placed it on the coffee table in front of Mrs. Hayley-Smith. I was proud of him. I couldn't have done it more dramatically myself. I waited for the start of guilt or flush of embarrassment Dad had talked about. I was disappointed.

Mrs. Hayley-Smith gave a small nod, picked up the box and said, "This is the medieval relic box we sent to the auction a couple of weeks ago." She held it up for the major to see.

"Isn't it, love?"

Startled, the major twitched, cleared his throat and said, "What? The box? Yes. Quite so."

"Is there some problem with it, Mr. Martin?" Mrs. Hayley-Smith said. "The auctioneer sent us a cheque. It was all in order, wasn't it, Dora?"

"Oh yes," gasped Dora.

"Good," Dad said. "Great."

Poor Dad. This was the tough part.

He leaned back, crossed his legs and tried to sound casual. "Mrs. Hayley-Smith, do you happen to remember where you got the box?" he asked. "It's an interesting piece. Have you any idea of its history?"

"Of course," said Mrs. Hayley-Smith. "It's been in the family a long time. It belonged to Sir Richard Fitzgilbert. My father, that is. I mean, that was. He passed away a few years ago." Her voice turned suspicious. "What's this all about, Mr. Martin?"

Dad told her about the boy at the auction. "Katy," he said, "show Mrs. Hayley-Smith the note."

I pulled it out of my pocket and handed it

over. Mrs. Hayley-Smith took it and held it out for the major and Dora to see. The major put on his glasses and leaned over Dora. Dora looked utterly wretched, like the dormouse squashed between the Mad Hatter and the White Rabbit.

Mrs. Hayley-Smith shrugged and handed the note back.

"Isn't it just a child's prank? As we used to say, 'Sticks and stones may break my bones, but words will never hurt me.' If I were you, I'd throw the paper away and forget all about it. That would be the sensible thing to do, now wouldn't it?" She spoke in a coaxing voice as if Dad were a little kid.

Dad leaned forward in a confidential way. "My wife is pregnant, Mrs. Hayley-Smith, and the incident upset her. She's having a lot of problems with her pregnancy. We'd like to return the box to its 'rightful owner,' as the note puts it."

Mrs. Hayley-Smith stared disbelievingly at Dad. "Return it? But you paid a lot of money for it," she said.

"Please don't misunderstand me," Dad said. "Naturally, I'd like to get my money back. But I'm prepared to make some arrangement — perhaps let the previous owner pay over time, in installments."

"Well, I'm sorry to disappoint you, but that's quite impossible, isn't it, Major? Dora? If we could afford to buy it, we wouldn't have sold it in the first place. Would we?"

"Oh no," said Dora. "Certainly not."

"Quite," said the major.

Dad looked down at his hands. Jenny and I weren't so tactful. We couldn't help looking around at all the other treasures in the room. Why couldn't the Hayley-Smiths sell something else and buy the relic box from Vivian and Dad?

Because they didn't want it back! Because it was cursed! "Excuse me, Mrs. Hayley-Smith," I said. "But do you have any children?" It was worth a try.

I thought I saw her give a little start, as if my question had taken her by surprise. Before I could be sure, she recovered her poise. "Yes," she said. "We have a married daughter. She lives in England — with her husband and two children. That's a photo of them on the table beside you." The photo showed a man and a woman with a boy of about six and a girl about eight. None of them looked anything like the family at the auction.

Mrs. Hayley-Smith stood up. She was hinting that the interview was over and we should leave. Dad packed up the relic box and politely thanked her for her time. I put the curse in my pocket. Dora the dormouse sprang to her feet.

"Mr. Martin," she squeaked, "if you are going back to Yorkville, could I be very rude and ask you for a ride? I . . . I'm supposed to meet a friend and I'm rather late. The buses on a Sunday are so . . . so . . ."

"Of course," Dad said. "No trouble at all. Where would you like to be dropped off?" Dad can be totally charming.

No wonder Dora had looked miserable during the interview. She was thinking if we didn't hurry and get out of there she'd never make her dinner date on time.

She gave Dad the name of a Yorkville restaurant. I think it was something like The Jumping Bean, but I've forgotten exactly. Anyway, we waited for her to get her coat — a brown fake fur — and then I let Jenny sit in the front seat with Dad while I got in the back with Dora. Jenny doesn't get to spend as much time with Dad as I do, because she's so busy with her music.

And, to tell the truth, I felt sorry for Dora, which just shows how wrong you can be. Or maybe not. Come to think of it, maybe my first instincts were the right ones.

Chapter 4

The Black Spot

Dora curled up on the seat and shyly looked at me. "Tell me, my dear, what will your father do now?"

I murmured something about going home for supper.

"Oh no," she said. "I mean about the relic box and its curse."

"I don't suppose there's much he can do," I said. "He'll have to take Mrs. Hayley-Smith's advice and forget about it."

"That does seem the best thing," Dora said. "I've found that Mrs. Hayley-Smith generally gives very good advice."

She sounded like a devoted little employee, the kind that went out of style about a hundred years ago. "Have you been with Mrs. Hayley-Smith for long, Miss . . . ?"

Dora looked kind of startled. Such a nervous

little mouse! "Please, call me Dora," she said. Then she smiled her timid little smile. "Yes," she said. "I suppose you could say we grew up together."

She must mean they'd been childhood friends and she'd naturally slipped into being Mrs. H's housekeeper. I wondered how I'd feel about being DeeDee's housekeeper. Yech!

Dora sighed. "Poor Mag!" she said.

I took it she meant Mrs. Hayley-Smith.

"There were just the two of them, you know," Dora went on. "Mag and her brother, Edward. Their father, Sir Edward Fitzgilbert, was an English baronet. Mag was the elder child, but when their father died, Edward inherited everything. That's the way the title is arranged."

"What a drag," I said. "For Mrs. Hayley-Smith I mean." It didn't seem fair to me.

Dora loved gossip. You could tell. "Oh, I agree," she chattered on. "Mag hasn't had an easy life. Her father was a . . . " she groped for words, ". . . a somewhat unusual man and she was always rather afraid of him. But Mag and her brother were very close. Edward was such a kind, gentle person, not a bit like his father. Then, about a year ago, Edward and his wife and their son, Ted, were killed in a car accident. Mag was devastated."

I tried to think of something sympathetic to say. All I came up with was, "How awful."

"Of course, there were death duties to pay,"

Dora said. "That's the way it is in England. Mrs. Hayley-Smith had to sell the family manor and its estate. It almost broke her heart." She sighed. "And now her house here in Toronto is always giving trouble. If it's not the pipes bursting, it's the roof leaking.

"Oh!" she gasped, so suddenly that she startled me. "I've just thought of something." She gazed at me, her eyes round. "Do you think that dreadful curse could be responsible? I mean, for the accident and losing the estate and the problems with the house and everything?"

"No," I said slowly, remembering the words in the note. "I don't think so. The curse wouldn't work on Mrs. Hayley-Smith because it only works on someone who isn't the rightful owner." It gave me the creeps to hear her take it so seriously. It seemed that the more I didn't want to believe in the curse, the more real it became.

I watched her face, to see the effect of what I said — the start of guilt, or whatever. Nothing!

Dora sank back in her seat. "Of course. How clever of you, my dear. Anyway, let us hope the curse is just nonsense, as Mrs. Hayley-Smith says. I should hate to think it could hurt anyone in your family."

Dad pulled up outside our house.

"Oh, is this where you live?" Dora asked. She sat up and rolled down the window. "What a pleasant street."

At any other time of year I would have agreed. But November doesn't bring out the best in our street. A thin fog had drifted in from the lake and hung like smoke in the pools of lamplight. The row of tall, Victorian houses stood shoulder to shoulder like soldiers whose uniforms have been rained on. Wet leaves and trickles of mud littered the sidewalk. Dora rolled down the window. "Which is your house, my dear?"

"Number 55," I said.

"Oh, you have such large numbers and right under the door lamp," Dora said enthusiastically. "What a sensible idea. Most people put their house numbers where no one can see them."

Dad turned to Dora in the back seat. "I thought I'd drop the girls off before I take you. I hope that's all right."

"Of course," Dora said. "It's most kind of you to bother. By the way, Mr. Martin, I do hope you have adequate insurance on that little relic box. Mrs. Hayley-Smith is always very careful about keeping up the insurance. A costly necessity, I'm afraid."

Dad looked sympathetic. "I know what you mean," he said. "My insurance bills are out of this world. Nothing short of daylight robbery."

Jenny and I usually use the back door, so we started to go down the path beside our house. We stopped to wave as Dad and Dora, still sympathizing with one another, drove away.

Mother and Adam, unable to hide their curiosity, were waiting for us.

"Did you have a nice afternoon?" Mother asked.

"Not nice exactly, but interesting," I answered.

"We still have no idea who the mystery boy is," Jenny said.

While Jenny told Mother and Adam about our visit to the Hayley-Smiths, I thought over what the dormouse had told me about Mrs. Hayley-Smith and her bad luck.

Could it have had anything to do with the curse? I asked myself. And a little voice inside me answered, you bet your life! In a weird sort of way, it was all beginning to make too much sense. No matter how innocent Mrs. Hayley-Smith pretended to be, she wasn't the rightful owner. The curse was working on her. That was why she decided to unload the relic box. And now Vivian had it!

I'd better pull myself together, I thought, or before I know it, I'll really start believing in that curse.

After Jenny finished telling about our afternoon, Adam scratched his beard and tried to look wise. "If you ask me, Mrs. Hayley-Smith is right. It was nothing but a child's prank. Vivian's a modern, intelligent woman. How can she let a few words on a piece of paper upset her? It's crazy stuff."

"Why don't you have a talk with her, Adam?" Jenny asked. "Tell her she's an idiot."

I couldn't tell by Jenny's face whether she was serious or not. Jenny's blonde hair and blue eyes make her look like an angel, but she sure doesn't act like one. By then, she'd forgiven Adam for marrying Mother, but she hadn't quite forgiven him for being allergic to our cat. Jenny adored Sam.

Sometimes I think Adam can't tell when he's being teased. At other times I think he only pretends to be dense, especially around Jenny, because he's so smart. Whichever it is, he didn't react. "Maybe I should talk to Vivian," he said, thoughtfully stroking his beard.

Mother looked alarmed. "No, Adam," she said. "I don't think we should interfere. The doctor will talk to Vivian. It can't be the first time he's met a pregnant woman with irrational fears."

"I don't think Vivian's being irrational," I said. "There could be something to this curse business."

I wasn't being totally serious. Partly I didn't like to hear them talking about Vivian as if she were either crazy or stupid, because she isn't. Mostly it was a sort of game — the kind DeeDee and I like to play to give ourselves the creeps.

"When Dad and Vivian took Jenny and me to England on holiday last summer, we went to the Roman baths in Bath," I said. "There was a sacred spring there dedicated to some goddess or other. I forget her name."

"Minerva," Jenny said.

"Okay, Minerva. Back in Roman times, a person who thought someone had done him wrong used to go to a scribe and pay him to write a curse on a thin piece of pewter. Then the person would throw the curse into Minerva's spring. The pool was full of curses when it was excavated. Curses must have worked, at least sometimes, or people wouldn't have gone on making them."

"Pure coincidence," Adam said. "In those days people didn't know much about disease. If you cursed someone and waited long enough, he'd get sick, or his pigs would, and you'd think it was because of your curse."

"Not pure coincidence," Jenny said. "If someone put a curse on William, he or she would make sure William got to hear about it. It's the power of suggestion. You can't separate mind from body."

"Sure," I said. "Remember in *Treasure Island* how the ex-pirate gets the black spot and dies? That's the trouble with Vivian. She's been given the black spot."

"If I remember correctly," Mother said, "the black spot was a warning to the pirate that his friends were out to get him. With friends like those, he probably died of a heart attack."

Mother knows a lot about books. She works in a library. "And I agree with Adam," she went on. "It's a lot of superstitious nonsense."

Mother and Adam are very practical people. They'd never lie awake shivering at some mysterious noise in the night. They'd get up and fix whatever it was that was making the noise. Or they'd pick up a baseball bat and stalk the luckless burglar. That's the way some people are — not much imagination. Maybe some people have too much. Like me.

Chapter 5
Cursed

The next Saturday was the day of the auditions. I couldn't eat breakfast because my stomach was already doing pirouettes. I had a terrible fear that I would forget my shoes, or lose a ribbon, or get a run in my tights, or drop the hairpins I needed to hold my hair in the regulation bun. I unpacked to make sure that I had a lot of extras of everything, and then had to re-pack.

Jenny looked disgusted. "What a worry-wart," she said. While I was fussing, I reached into the top drawer of my dresser and there it was — the piece of paper with the curse on it. I re-read it and collapsed onto the bed in mock-despair. "Oh no!" I wailed. "I'm going to screw up, I know I am. I'll never get a solo. I'll be lucky if I get any part at all. I'm cursed."

Jenny grabbed the paper. "Stop it," she ordered. "You're not being funny. Besides, this has nothing to do with you. It's for Vivian."

"It says, 'Cursed be thee and thine,'" I said stubbornly. "We're hers."

"We are not," Jenny snapped. "We're Dad's kids, not Vivian's."

Trust Jenny to point that out.

"Vivian thinks we're hers," I said. "She really cares about us. I guess it's because she doesn't have much family of her own — no brothers or sisters or anything. When she married Dad she thought she was getting instant family."

"Whoever wrote the curse didn't know that," Jenny insisted. "It means Vivian and her blood relatives. That's an old-fashioned way of putting it. These days we talk about genes, not blood, but you get the idea."

I nodded. Maybe Jenny was right. The person who laid the curse on the relic box couldn't know that Vivian had stepdaughters. He thought he'd covered all the bases by saying "thee and thine." Then I thought of something else.

"Jenny! I cried. "What about Vivian's mother's accident?"

"What about it?"

"Vivian's mother isn't her mother," I said. "She's her stepmother. Her own mother died when Vivian was a child."

Jenny pushed me down so that I was lying on the bed.

"Relax," she said. "You just said Vivian's mother had an accident — and you're right, that's all it was."

I was glad Jenny was being so sensible. I knew she was right. It was just that darn audition making me nervous. "I've got to go," I said, struggling up off the bed. "I've got to warm up."

"You've got half an hour at least before you have to go," Jenny said. "Listen to me. I know how to help you get a part." She made me do muscle-relaxing exercises and then imagine myself dancing perfectly at the audition. It's called imaging. Athletes use it to improve their performances. Jenny said her teacher had used the same technique with her before a piano recital. Jenny says the powers of the mind are truly amazing.

During the auditions I totally forgot about the curse. I was too busy concentrating on doing my best.

When I went to class next day the results were up. My name was at the top of the list! I had the principal role in the whole ballet. I couldn't believe it. Neither could some of the senior girls, but they were very nice about it. After class I rushed home, grabbed Jenny and whirled her around in a victory dance. "Your system worked," I whooped. "How is a mystery to me, but who cares. I imaged myself right into the principal part. So much for that stupid curse," I said. "It doesn't work."

35

Next day Dad phoned to say that Vivian had to go to hospital. She had something called pregnancy edema and she'd have to stay in hospital until the baby was born in about two months.

"Now that could be the curse," I said later to Jenny. "It doesn't work on us, but it might work on Vivian."

"Katy," said Jenny, "anyone can get sick." She looked thoughtful. "I'm not saying there's no connection. But if there is, it's all in Vivian's head."

"You're always criticising Vivian," I said. "You never did like her."

"I like her a lot better now she's become a nut-case," Jenny said. "It's hard to like somebody who appears to be perfect. Anyway, it's partly your fault that I didn't like her before. Ask my shrink."

After Mother married Adam, Jenny had agreed to go to a counsellor to help her get over Dad's and Mother's new marriages. The counsellor had done a good job. At least I'd thought so till then.

"My fault!"

"Yes," Jenny said. "Before Vivian married Dad, you always looked up to me. Then, suddenly, Mother was all tied up with Adam, and you and Dad were like two planets revolving around Vivian's star. No wonder I was jealous."

"We weren't. I mean, I was not," I yelped. I felt about six notches lower than a worm. I'd never meant to hurt Jenny. "It doesn't matter," Jenny went on. "That's all water under the bridge, as my shrink says. Anyway, I agree with you. If Dad wants Vivian to have a healthy baby, he should humour her and give the box back to its previous owner."

"How?" I asked.

Jenny didn't know.

"Ask your shrink," I said. "Maybe she's got some more bright ideas."

Dad said Vivian would like to have visitors, so Jenny and I went to see her at the hospital.

"It's so boring here," Vivian said.

She was lying on the bed, hands clasped, doing nothing. There wasn't a sign of her old sparkle. She looked dull and plain. Her face was pale and puffy. I was shocked.

"Where's your knitting?" Jenny asked. "Did you finish the little jacket you were making?"

"I don't feel like knitting right now," Vivian said, not looking Jenny in the eye.

I guessed why. She felt that knitting for the baby was tempting fate. I often felt the same way — that you shouldn't plan for something you want very much because it's tempting fate not to let you have it. Vivian might seem cool and sophisticated, but that was just the tip of the iceberg.

"Think positive," Jenny told her. "As you knit, imagine your baby, healthy and beautiful, wearing the little jacket you're making."

Jenny and her "power of positive thinking" again! I suddenly noticed how grown up she sounded. She talked to Vivian as if they were the same age. I felt the way I used to feel when I was a little kid and Jenny went off to play with her own friends and told me I couldn't go along.

"I've tried to be sensible, Jenny," Vivian said. "But there's a part of me that won't listen to reason. A snake in the grass that rears up and whispers that everything is going wrong. It scares me. The words of that curse seem to be engraved on the backs of my eyes."

Jenny nodded, as if she understood. "Vivian, you must really try to see the baby, happy and healthy in your arms. Imagine the colour of its hair and its eyes. I guess you'll have to decide whether it's going to be a girl or a boy."

Vivian hesitated a while, then she said quietly, "I know what it is. It showed on the tests. Should I tell you?"

"Yes," Jenny yipped.

I wasn't sure. It felt a bit like tempting fate again, but I went along with Jenny.

"It's a boy," Vivian said.

For a minute the shine came back into her eyes, her face glowed and she looked so happy she made me want to cry.

Jenny grinned. "What did I tell you? Katy, you owe me five bucks. Pay up," she said.

She hadn't changed that much. Still the same little moneybags!

Vivian's smile faded and her anxious look came back.

"If only we could find that boy from the auction," she said, "I'd willingly give him the box. I don't care any more about the money we'd lose."

"Adam says curses don't work," I said. I thought it might make her feel better. "He says it's all coincidence."

Vivian shook her head. "It's too easy to put things down to coincidence. I believe there are forces we don't yet understand. What about people who have premonitions of disaster? Or people who know the minute something terrible happens to a loved one who is far away? Perhaps we should admit we don't yet know the full power of the human brain. I wish we could find that boy. He was such an unhappy child."

Unhappy! How could she call that little monster unhappy? Only Vivian would see anything good in that kid. She even liked me and Jenny when we were being brats about her marrying Dad. She'd understood how we felt. Vivian was going to be a great mother.

"Your father will be heartbroken if anything happens to the baby," Vivian went on. "And I want to make him happy. He misses you girls so much."

"But he sees us all the time," Jenny said.

"It's not the same," Vivian said. "He feels like a part-time father now that he has to share you with Adam."

I was stunned. I'd never guessed Dad felt that way. No wonder he wanted another child.

As Jenny and I travelled home on the bus, I said, "I'm glad it's going to be a boy. That way, Dad'll have one family with daughters in it — us. And he'll have a second family with a son in it. He won't get us muddled."

Jenny said impatiently, "Vivian had better get her act together pretty soon, or Dad won't be getting another child, however much he wants one."

Chapter 6

The Burglary

The next Sunday it was Mother's and Adam's turn to spend time with Jenny and me. Mother is a fitness nut. You'd think a daily ballet class would satisfy her, but to count with Mother exercise has to be done in the fresh air.

"You're both so pale," she often complains. "You spend far too much time indoors." She's always on Jenny's case. "You're getting round shoulders from all that piano practice," she says, her face puckered with worry.

"Oh, Mother, do we have to go skiing?" Jenny moaned.

Jenny's idea of exercise is a day in bed flicking over the pages of a novel. "It's so cold outside."

All Mother said was, "Get your skis."

She and Adam took us to the Don River Valley where there's a trail running through the trees beside the river. The day was bright and crisp. There had been a heavy frost overnight and the trees along the creek were crusty white. When the sun came out, it danced along the branches, dislodging ice crystals as it went.

Mother was right. There was something to be said for exercising out of doors and, unlike Jenny, I enjoy using my body. I swished along in front, skimmed down a hill and, there, at the bottom, I saw him.

The boy from the auction sale! He was skiing along the trail ahead of me.

At first I couldn't believe it, but as I came closer he looked at me over his shoulder. I'd have known those eyes anywhere. I stopped dead, rooted to the spot.

"Katy. Move!"

Jenny's panicky yell seemed to echo from far, far away. I turned to see what was wrong. Her skis rattled against mine as she swooshed to a stop and fell backwards.

"What's wrong with you, Katy?" she asked angrily, struggling to stand up. "You know I'm no good at stopping. Didn't you hear me yell?"

"Jenny," I whispered, "Jenny, he's here. The boy from the auction. Look." I turned to point him out. He was gone. I clutched at Jenny. "Did you see him?" I asked.

"Who?" Jenny, still furious, was dusting snow off herself. "That boy. The one ahead of us."

"I didn't see anybody — except you blocking the trail. Why can't you warn people when you're going to stop all of a sudden?"

Mother and Adam skiied down to us. "Why are you two standing about?" Mother asked. "You'll get cold."

As soon as she said it, I realized I felt as cold as ice. My teeth began to chatter.

"Mother," Jenny said, "Katy's not well. She's seeing things. I think we should take her home."

"Jenny," Mother scolded, "you're always looking for excuses not to exercise. Katy's cold because she's standing around."

Adam looked at my chattering teeth. "You look a little tired," he said sympathetically. "Would you like me to go first? It takes more energy to break trail."

He set off, with Mother and Jenny following. Deep in thought, I came last. How come Jenny hadn't seen that boy? Had I been seeing things? But he'd seemed so real. Come to that, so do the people you see in dreams — until you wake up. Perhaps he'd put a spurt on and vanished around a curve. If he was jet-propelled, that is. I'd been setting a pretty good pace.

I wasn't enjoying myself any more. The snow reflected the sunlight with a harsh brightness that hurt my eyes, and I couldn't get warm. I was glad when Mother and Adam decided we should go home.

At home there was another shock waiting.

The cupboards and drawers in the living-room were wide open and our belongings were all higgledy-piggledy, as though someone had been rummaging through them. For a moment we stood there, all four of us, with our mouths open. Then Adam took charge.

"Out," he ordered. "Pam, girls, wait outside. I'll look around. The burglar might still be here."

Jenny and I huddled together near the open front door, ready to run. (For help, if Adam needed any, Jenny said afterwards.)

Mother, brandishing one ski pole as a weapon, began to creep upstairs after Adam. Then she thought better of it. She went to the telephone and dialed the police instead.

When the detective came, he shook his head sadly. "They get younger every year," he said. "Look at that muddy footprint on the kitchen floor. It's small enough for a ten-year-old." Then he looked at Jenny and me.

We're not exactly big for our ages and he made us stand next to the footprint and measure our feet against it. Jenny's was too big. Mine was about right.

"You have very small feet," he said.

I remembered reading somewhere about how the shape of your earlobes is supposed to show if you have criminal tendencies. Maybe having small feet was a sign, too. I felt like a juvenile delinquent.

"I can't help it," I said, guiltily. "I take after my father."

That happens to be true. Dad has very small feet for his size. Adam has hoofs like an elephant. The inspector looked at Adam. Embarrassed, Adam shuffled his feet. The inspector glanced sideways at me. I could see he thought I was either a liar or a smart aleck. None of us felt like explaining.

The detective looked around to see how the burglar had got in. "That tree," he said, "outside the bedroom. There are twigs in the bedroom. I reckon the intruder climbed the tree and came in through the window." He turned to Jenny. "Was the window open?"

Jenny nodded. "A little bit." She never closed that window. Mother was always getting after her about it. B.A. — before Adam — she always kept it open for Sam. Sam used to climb out, sit in the branches of the tree, view the world for a while, then climb back inside. After Sam went to live with Dad and Vivian, Jenny kept her window open in case he wandered home and wanted to come in.

How could a burglar climb a tree at the front of the house in broad daylight and open the window enough to climb in? Our windows are old and sticky. It didn't make much sense to me. "Wouldn't someone have seen him?" I asked.

"You'd be surprised what people don't see,"

the detective said. "And what makes you think it's a him? Female chauvinist, eh?"

That detective thought he knew it all. But if you were a burglar, and a small one, I doubt very much if you could balance on a branch and heave Jenny's window open.

I went to do a bit of investigating of my own. The back door key, which we keep hanging on a nail high up in the milk chute, was in its usual place; but the burglar could have used it and then put it back.

"Bring your list of missing items to the station when you've had time to go through everything," the detective said. But it was really bizarre. We couldn't come up with a list of missing items. Nothing was gone. The police said the burglar must have been interested in something special.

"The relic box," I said to Jenny.

"Why would he look for it in our house?" Jenny asked. "Vivian and Dad were the ones who bought it."

"But I was with them," I said. "The boy might think it was here."

Jenny gave me a hard, searching look. "In the first place, how would he know where you live? In the second, didn't you say you saw him when we were out skiing?"

"I only thought I saw him. You said so yourself." I gazed into space. "It was probably some sort of premonition I had. Otherwise, why would I have felt so scared when I saw — thought I saw — the boy? Maybe I'm psychic."

"Spelled S-I-C-K?" said Jenny.

I ignored her. I wasn't sure whether to feel proud of my new gift, or scared out of my mind. Either way, it made me rather interesting, I thought, and not an object of fun.

"You don't understand," I told Jenny huffily. "Some of us are more sensitive than others. More tuned in to the cosmic unconscious."

"Unconscious is right," muttered Jenny irritably.

I was getting a little tired of everbody being so darn sensible. In fact, the more people disagreed with me, the more I started thinking there really was something to the curse. "Maybe that boy has supernatural powers," I said. "I'll bet he really did make that guy break a vase at the auction sale. And now I'm picking up his thought waves. That's how his curse operates." I was really getting carried away. A shiver ran up my spine. It wasn't totally unpleasant, but it would've been a lot more fun if DeeDee had been there instead of my wet-blanket sister.

"Katy, cut it out," Jenny said, wagging her finger under my nose. "You've got to stop believing in this curse business. It could be dangerous."

Chapter 7

An Accident

It was our very first rehearsal for the special ballet performance. Nigel Plume, one of the senior boys, was my partner. He wasn't very pleased about it. I was too young for him. Every chance he got, he'd go and stand at the practice bar with his back to me. The studio was lined with mirrors and I could see his reflection as he laughed and whispered with the older girls.

Nigel had dark curly hair and green eyes. He thought he was God's gift to ballerinas. Unfortunately for me our special teacher, Miss Olga, seemed to agree with him.

"Verrry good, Nigel," she cooed, rolling her r's. When she looked at me, all she did was roll her eyes. "Yes, Nigel. Verrry, verrry good. You are so strrrong."

Nigel's chest swelled with pride. He decided to show Miss Olga just how strong he was. The next thing I knew, I was in the air and coming down for a landing — a crash landing. Nigel's head caught me right in the face.

Blinded by pain, I clutched my nose. I felt sure it was broken — along with my hopes. My nose would swell to humungous proportions. Miss Olga certainly wouldn't want a prima ballerina who looked like Miss Piggy in a tutu. Dizzyingly, stars whirled in my head. For a minute, I thought I was going to faint.

Then, to my amazement, the pain stopped. My face went numb. I decided my nose wasn't broken after all. When I opened my eyes I saw Nigel looking at me, stricken with remorse. I wiped my eyes, forced a smile, and stood beside him, ready to begin again. Miss Olga had no time for wimps. Besides, I wanted to prove I wasn't injured. Otherwise, I'd be out and my understudy would be in.

Nigel and I had to do leaps across the studio. I'd done them hundreds of times in class. I enjoyed the feeling of lightness in my body, almost as if I were flying. Leaps were my best thing. This was my big chance to impress Miss Olga.

"Pride comes before a fall." I'd heard that somewhere. The next thing I knew, I was on the floor, in a heap. I was so embarrassed I leaped to my feet. My right knee felt as if it had come apart and my leg collapsed under me.

As I squirmed on the floor in agony, I knew I

couldn't fake my way out of this one. My leg was seriously injured. My dreams of stardom were shattered. Why did this have to happen? I asked myself. Why now? Why me?

That was when I remembered the curse.

That's got to be what caused this, I thought. I looked up and caught sight of Nigel's reflection in one of the mirrors. His expression was a mixture of disbelief and pity.

I was in a lot of pain. Suddenly, the glass shimmered. When my vision cleared, instead of Nigel, I saw the boy from the auction. I gasped and swung my head around to look at him directly. He was nowhere in the room.

Then everything in the studio faded. I could hear voices faintly in the background, but I couldn't make out what they were saying. Only the mocking face of the boy was still as clear as day. I couldn't take my eyes off him. And while I gazed, something really horrible happened. The boy changed. He grew older. His face became the face of an old man, wrinkled and sallow. He wasn't a pleasant old man. His eyes were hooded, his mouth thin and downturned. His body was stooped and he leaned on a cane that was almost as gnarled as his fingers. I screamed.

"Katy! Katy! My poor, poor child." Tearfully, Miss Lightfoot bent over me, blocking out the awful image in the mirror.

I'll spare you the story of my operation. After

a few days I was ready to go home, with my leg in a cast. All I could see of my leg were my toes wriggling at the far end. The doctor came for a farewell chat.

"How soon do I get the cast off?" I asked.

"I'll see you in about six weeks," he said.

"Six weeks!" I cried. "I can't wait that long. I'm a dancer. I'll get out of shape."

"I'm sorry, Katy," he said, "but after the cast comes off you'll need physiotherapy. You won't be dancing for quite a while."

Something in his face worried me. "How long?" I asked. He looked at Mother who had taken the day off work to bring me home from the hospital. Mother straightened her back, lifted her chin and put on her efficient look. My heart sank.

"I think we should be honest with you, Katy," she said. "You must try to be brave. I'm afraid the doctor doesn't know if you'll be able to dance again."

"Not dance! Not ever?"

If you've never had a really fierce ambition to do something, you probably don't know how it feels to be told you can't do it. But I'd already spent years training to be a dancer. It was all I'd ever wanted to do. Dancing was my real life. Everything else came second.

The image of the boy swam in front of me. It was his fault. I knew it.

"It isn't fair," I cried. "Why me? Why couldn't you go after somebody else?"

The instant I'd said it, I wished I could take it back. What if he took me at my word and went after Dad or Jenny? I freaked out. "That's not what I meant," I cried. Face down, I pounded the pillow. "Go away. Go away and leave us all alone."

"Katy," Mother said, shaking my shoulder. "Katy, stop it. Stop it at once."

A nurse came and stuck a needle into my thigh.

"The needle will calm her down," I heard the doctor say. I had news for him. It would take more than a needle to calm me down. I sat up. "I want to talk to Dad," I said.

"All right, Katy." Mother sounded as though she were trying to humour a two-year-old. "Why don't we go home and get you settled, then I'll ask your father to come over."

While I was waiting for Dad, Adam and Jenny came home. When Jenny saw me, her eyes filled with tears.

"Oh, Katy," she wailed, "you look terrible."

She had a point. Not only was I wearing a cast, my face was black and blue from its collision with Nigel's head.

"Thanks," I said. "Thanks a heap." But I knew she meant well. The words just hadn't come out right.

"For goodness sake, Jenny," Mother scolded. "It's not the end of the world. She'll be back to normal in a month or two." Mother doesn't believe in offering sympathy. She thinks it makes people feel sorry for themselves and they get better faster without it. She never fussed over me or Jenny when we were little kids. "Up you get," she'd say when we fell over. I must admit we never got scared and howled our heads off the way some kids do.

"Can I get you anything?" Adam asked. "A glass of water, perhaps?"

It was his way of saying he felt sorry for me, without going against Mother. He never interfered with the way she brought us up. I guess he figured we were her kids, not his. "No thanks, Adam," I said. Mother had already set a glass and a jug of water on the coffee table in front of the sofa where I was lying with my leg up, like one of those silent movie stars. Except that I didn't feel like a movie star, silent or otherwise.

Adam shifted his weight from one foot to the other. I could see he felt useless. All of a sudden it struck me that maybe he sometimes felt left out around Mother and Jenny and me — the way I sometimes did around Dad and Vivian.

I really wanted to make him feel better, so I decided to take him into my confidence. "You know who caused all this, don't you, Adam? It's that boy I told you about — the one at the auction — the one who put his curse on us." I should've saved my breath.

Adam drew up a chair and sat down beside

me. He looked at me gravely. "Katy, you don't seriously believe that, do you? Everything is subject to natural laws. Your accident was pure coincidence. Nigel was careless, that's all. There's a perfectly simple reason for what happened."

"Of course there is," said Mother. "Miss Lightfoot shouldn't have given you the principal part. You're too young."

"No, I'm not," I said. The tears came to my eyes. "And it's probably the last chance I'll ever have to be a prima ballerina." I couldn't help feeling sorry for myself.

Adam patted my shoulder. "Don't worry, Katy," he said. "You're young and strong. Your knee will heal. You'll be as good as new in a few months."

Not a chance. Not with that curse hanging over my head. I didn't say it out loud. What was the use? Mother and Adam weren't the sort of people you could talk to about things like witches and curses.

When Dad arrived, they tactfully made some excuse about making supper and left us alone.

"I have to practice," Jenny said. "Talk to you later, Dad." Jenny was being tactful too.

Dad put his arms around me. "Poor baby," he said, stroking my hair. "Poor little Katy. If only it could have happened to me instead of to you."

I knew he meant it. He'd always been so proud of Jenny and me. He came to all Jenny's piano recitals and to every performance I danced in. Now he'd never be able to feel proud of me again. I leaned against his shoulder and dripped tears all over the expensive Italian sweater Vivian had bought him. "I wish there was something I could do," he said.

"There is something you can do." I sniffed hard and wiped my wet face with the back of my hand.

"Tell me." Dad handed me his clean, white handkerchief.

"You've got to find that boy from the auction and get him to lift his curse. He's the one who's causing all this trouble. He's some sort of witch."

Dad got up and began to pace — the way he does when he's upset. His forehead was creased and his eyes were baggy underneath, as though he hadn't been sleeping much.

"I've tried to find the boy, Katy. You know I have. I've asked Mrs. Hayley-Smith for help. I've even had an ad running in the personals column of the newspaper. 'If the rightful owner of the relic box wishes to have it returned, he or she should contact Robert Martin, etcetera.'

"The only replies I've had are from nosey parkers and cranks. I wish I could find whoever wrote that curse. I'd like to give him a piece of my mind. But what else can I do?" He sighed and rubbed his forehead. "I wish you and Vivian could believe that this so-called curse can't possibly hurt you, unless you let it."

Dad sounded almost as bad as Adam. I was disappointed in him. "I see. So you think Vivian and I are crazy," I said. "That's it, is it?"

"No, Katy, that's not it."

Dad isn't the most patient person in the world.

"In all of us, and I include myself, there's a superstitious part that still believes in bad luck and curses or hexes," he went on. "It's part of our inheritance from our ancient ancestors. And whoever wrote that curse knew it. He or she was mean enough to take advantage of other people's irrational fears."

"Sure, Dad," I said, bitterly. "It's all in the mind, like Jenny says."

But I hadn't even been thinking about the curse at rehearsal, so how could it have made me so nervous I had two accidents in one day? Without warning, I'd been struck down. Me, Katy Martin, who'd never had even a minor dancing injury before. My body seemed made for ballet. Then, out of the blue, I might never dance again. Nothing could convince me any more that the curse wasn't hurting us somehow. Vivian had to be right. There was something out of the ordinary going on.

The next day I hopped along on my crutches to the library and looked at every book on witches that I could find.

None of the books mentioned a witch who was

still a child. The youngest were teenage girls. I read on. In the old days people believed that witches were able to change into other forms of life. Shape-changing, it was called. And they flew around on sticks. It didn't have to be a broomstick.

Well, on the day I wrecked my knee, the boy had changed into an old man right before my eyes. And the old man had a cane. It all fitted. Dad had said the curse wasn't written by a child. So the boy wasn't a boy at all. He was a male witch, a warlock, who sometimes took the form of a boy.

A lot of the stuff I read was pretty gross. They used to give witches a hard time. Burning at the stake was only part of it. They'd throw suspected witches into a pond or lake. If they floated or could swim, that meant they were guilty. If they drowned, they were innocent! What we call nowadays a "no-win situation."

I didn't enjoy reading about how witches were treated. But I didn't like finding out about what they were supposed to do, either. The only comforting thought was that at least now I knew what I was up against.

Chapter 8

Liar!

Vivian wasn't like Mother and Adam. She understood totally how I felt about my accident. She'd wanted to be a dancer, but she'd grown too tall. She knew there was such a thing as bad luck, or fate being against you, or getting cursed, and other things you can't explain. She didn't try to tell me everything would be okay. She just put her arms around me.

"I wish I'd never seen that horrible box," she said, tears running down her cheeks. "I feel so guilty — as if your accident was all my fault."

The next time Jenny and I went to see her, she was trying to knit, but all she was really doing was twisting the wool around her fingers.

"Your father's always rushing from the shop to the hospital, and back again," she said. "I wish he wouldn't drive when he's tired. That's how accidents happen."

"Now that I don't have ballet any more, I could help Dad in the shop," I said.

"You've got to be kidding!" said Jenny.

"Could you, Katy?" Vivian asked eagerly. "Your father's hired a part-time sales clerk, but Mrs. Menzies doesn't know much about antiques. You could help answer customers' questions." She turned to Jenny. "You'd be surprised how much Katy knows."

Modestly, I blushed. I'd always taken a lot of interest in the antique business. I love old things and usually I enjoy meeting the people who come into the shop.

"But Katy looks as if she got run over by a truck," Jenny said.

The bruises on my face had faded from purple to blue, with a nice greenish yellow round the edges. What with that, and my crutches, I really didn't want to meet people. It was bad enough having to go to school. But I couldn't help remembering Dora's story about Mrs. Hayley-Smith's brother's fatal car accident. I didn't want anything like that to happen to Dad!

"I'll help on late nights and on Saturdays," I said.

The next Saturday, I was sitting at the back of the shop waiting for customers. Sam was lying on my lap, purring. Good old Sam didn't care how I looked. Mrs. Menzies, the new clerk, was sitting at Dad's desk, working at the accounts. The shop bell tinkled and I looked up to see who had come in. I almost fell off my chair with surprise.

There stood Dora the dormouse. She was wearing a brown fake fur hat and brown woollen gloves, as well as her fake fur coat, and as she stood in the doorway hanging her head, she looked more like a dormouse than ever.

I shifted Sam off my lap and onto the chair, took up my crutches and went to help her.

"Good afternoon," she said in her timid, breathless voice, looking at me from under her eyelashes. Then she recognized me. "Oh, my dear! Whatever happened to you?"

"I had an accident," I mumbled.

Little Dora looked so sorry for me I thought she might burst into tears. "And your mother, my dear, how is she?" she asked anxiously.

"She's very well, thank you," I answered. Maybe she thought Mother and I had been going a few rounds in the boxing ring!

She looked relieved. "And the baby?" she asked. "It hasn't been born yet, has it?"

The light dawned. She was talking about Vivian. Dad had talked about "my wife" when we visited the Hayley-Smiths and he'd introduced Jenny and me as his daughters. All of it true, but you couldn't expect other people to know about our bizarre family. I had to tell her that Vivian was my stepmother, not my mother.

"Oh," she said, licking her lips. "I see. So your

father doesn't live with you in that lovely, Victorian house?"

"No," I said. "Dad and Vivian live here, in the apartment above the shop."

Dora the dormouse loved gossip. She gathered it up and stuffed herself with it. I guessed it was because she didn't have a very interesting life of her own and she had to live on other people's crumbs, the way some people get involved in the lives of soap-opera characters. She wanted to know all about my accident, and about why Vivian had to be in hospital.

I didn't want to be rude, but I didn't want to answer a lot of personal questions either. As soon as I decently could, I asked if I could help her.

"Oh," she said, "I hope so. I brought this picture. Mrs. Hayley-Smith wondered if your father might sell it for us. He's such a charming man." She laid a large, gilt-framed painting on the counter.

"I'm afraid Dad isn't in just now," I said. The painting was one of those English hunting scenes, with people dressed in red jackets capering around on horseback and blowing horns — not the sort of thing I care for.

The dormouse stood beside me and studied the picture. "I wonder if it might be worth a thousand dollars," she said. "The artist was famous in Victorian England. It's a very good painting, you know."

It sure didn't look like a very good painting. It looked like a very ordinary painting. I wondered if the dormouse was lying. Not that I cared. English hunting scenes were popular, and huge gilded frames were worth a fortune.

"We need the money quite badly," Dora said. She gazed at the picture and sighed. "Mag hates to part with any of the family heirlooms. She feels it's her duty to pass them on to the next generation. That's right, don't you think?"

I didn't want Dora to take the picture away. Dad would give his eyeteeth for a client like Mrs. Hayley-Smith.

"Well," I said, "a person can't keep everything. I mean, the house would get really crowded, wouldn't it? And I'm pretty sure the picture's worth a thousand dollars. Why don't you leave it here? My father could phone you tomorrow to discuss the details."

I pulled out a form from the shelf behind the counter. "I'll give you a receipt for the picture and leave a note for Dad."

"My dear, do you mind if I wait a while in case your father comes back?" the dormouse asked. "I'd like to look around. You have some interesting things here."

I said I didn't mind and went to help Mrs. Menzies while Dora amused herself looking at everything, and I do mean everything. She not only dressed like a mouse, she moved like one, in short bursts. She'd whiffle her whiskers over something then scuttle somewhere else.

Most of our customers like Sam. Dora didn't. She kept her distance and watched him out of the corner of her eye. Typical mouse, I thought.

"Your cat bears a striking resemblance to the cat on the relic box," she said, looking around. "I don't see the box anywhere. Has your father sold it?"

"No. They keep it in their apartment," I said.

So that was it — Dora was scared of Sam because he reminded her of the curse.

She hung around, fidgeting. Dad didn't come back. Finally, it was closing time.

"I'll do as you suggested and leave the picture," the dormouse said. "Perhaps you could give me my receipt."

I filled it out. Received from . . . "Is Mag short for Margaret?" I asked Dora who was hovering near my shoulder.

"Oh no," she said. "It's short for Magpie."

I couldn't believe it. "Magpie!" I said. "You mean her parents actually called her Magpie? How cruel!" I shouldn't have spoken like that to a customer, but I couldn't help it. "Oh, I don't think her father meant to be cruel," Dora said. "He liked magpies. He said they were handsome, intelligent birds and he hoped his daughter would be like one." She sighed. "I'm afraid she was a great disappointment to him."

I couldn't see why. She'd lived up to her name. Sitting there in that house full of treasures, not wanting to part with a single one. I wished Dora wouldn't be so nice about the Hayley-Smiths. Nobody should be that devoted. I almost stopped thinking of her as Dora, the dormouse, in favour of Dora, the doormat. I finished filling in the receipt, signed it and gave it to her. "Dad'll phone you tomorrow," I said.

"You will mention to him that the painting is a very good one, won't you, my dear?" she said. "And please be sure to tell him to ask for Dora when he phones. I take care of all Mrs. Hayley-Smith's business matters."

Dad has a lot of reference books so, just for the heck of it, I decided to check out the artist. Finally I found something — a small paragraph in a very large book.

"Minor artist, achieved brief popularity in Victorian England, mainly because of subjects depicted. Little artistic merit."

How come Dora didn't know that? I bet she did. I bet she was saying just what Mrs. Hayley-Smith had told her to say. Mrs. Hayley-Smith was a total liar.

Next day I checked to see that Dad had phoned her. I knew he had a lot on his mind because of Vivian and the Christmas shopping rush.

"Yes," Dad said, "I phoned. Mrs. Hayley-

Smith answered, but I asked for Dora, as you said I should." He looked thoughtful. "Something about Mrs. Hayley-Smith puzzles me. Over the years I've spent a lot of time in England. I'd expect the daughter of a baronet to speak with a private school accent — upper crust and all that. Mrs. Hayley-Smith sounds like someone quite ordinary."

"Maybe her father couldn't afford to send her to a private school," I said. Or maybe he was too mean, I thought. To me he sounded a total nerd.

Dad nodded. "A lot of those aristocratic families have nothing much left but their titles. Dora said the Hayley-Smiths would take a thousand dollars for the picture. I'll see if I can get more than that for them, but I didn't promise anything. It's better to give the client a pleasant surprise than a nasty shock."

Dad could easily have sold the picture for more than a thousand dollars and kept the extra profit. But he wouldn't do that. Dad's an honest businessman.

I love my dad and, after I'd spoken to him, the words of the curse floated into my mind. "Thee and thine shall suffer and perish." I went cold all over. Jenny says I'm a real worry-wart. But nobody was more "thine" to Vivian than Dad, so how could I help worrying about him?

Chapter 9

Wild Goose Chase

In spite of my crutches, every day after school I went to work at Dad and Vivian's shop. Dad was glad of my help. He wanted to keep the shop open evenings over the Christmas season.

Mother and Adam said that it was a good idea for me to work.

"Keeping busy will help you not to miss your dancing," Mother said.

"Vivian needs your father around," Adam said. "Having you at the shop makes it easier for him to spend time with her."

What they really meant was, "Working in the shop will keep you away from Vivian." They thought she'd flipped over the curse and they were afraid the craziness might be catching, like measles. Of course, they didn't want to say so because that wouldn't have been polite. Even

Jenny gave me a hard time. "You're not your usual self lately," she said. "I think you have hidden anxieties. Why don't you ask Mother if you can talk to my shrink?"

"I don't need a shrink," I said. "I need someone who understands curses, like a genuine witch doctor. But where do I find one of those in Toronto?"

"Try the yellow pages," Jenny said.

I ignored her sarcasm. I even looked in the yellow pages. There were no witch doctors listed.

"Ask a clergyman," my friend DeeDee advised. "They sometimes do exorcisms." She hugged herself and giggled.

"Exorcisms are for ghosts," I said. "The boy who cursed us isn't a ghost. He's a witch."

DeeDee giggled again.

"Listen," I said. "This is no joke. Look what he did to me."

DeeDee glanced down at my cast and immediately sobered up. "But I thought witches were female, and kind of old," she said. "Not always," I countered. "This one's a male. Otherwise known as a warlock. And he's not necessarily young. You can't always go by appearances," I added mysteriously. "He's also dangerous — maybe even a potential murderer."

DeeDee's eyes got big and round. "You're kidding," she said in an awed whisper.

"No, I'm not," I said. "I wish I could find him."

My wish was about to be granted.

One Saturday afternoon about three weeks before Christmas, Mrs. Menzies was talking to a customer. I was sitting at the back of the shop resting the weight of my cast on a stool when Sam lifted his head from his chair and gave one of those bloodcurdling yowls that cats usually save for other cats.

Startled, I looked up.

The witch boy stood in the doorway. His hands were in the pockets of his black leather jacket as he leaned against the door frame, watching me. I couldn't move. I even held my breath. Breathing might make him disappear, or change — the way he had before. Remembering that hideous image in the mirror made my mouth turn dry and my heart pound.

He smiled — not in his usual sneering way, but as if he wanted to talk to me. Then he took his left hand out of his pocket and wiggled his fingers in a little wave.

Slowly I stood up and reached for my crutches. The boy turned and sauntered out of the shop. I caught a whiff of damp leather. This time I was sure he was real.

"Wait!" I called, as I clumped after him. "I want to talk to you."

He didn't stop. Instead, he ran a little way down the street, glancing back to see if I was following.

"Hey," I yelled. "Stop. Come back."

He stopped, turned and made a face. "Can't catch me," he called. Then he grinned and began to skip along the sidewalk like a mischievous little boy wanting to tease an older sister. I wasn't in a playful mood. Not after what he'd done. But I decided to play along. Crutches or no crutches, I couldn't let him get away.

Mrs. Menzies ran after me into the street. She called something about where was I going and shouldn't I take my jacket. I ignored her. I had to. I didn't dare take my eyes off the boy for one second. It would be too easy to lose him.

He hopped, skipped and jumped along, weaving his way through the Christmas shoppers. Now and again he stopped, laughing as he peeped out of some doorway, or around a lamp post to see if he'd lost me. He hadn't. Thanks to all those ballet classes, I was in good shape. I swung along on my crutches like some three-legged creature from an alien world. Out of the corner of my eye, I caught indignant stares from the people I almost ran down. Most scuttled out of my way like frightened chickens then watched, clucking angrily, as I raced past. I remember the sound of parcels tumbling to the sidewalk as I jostled someone. But I never took my eyes off the boy.

How long did he mean to go on? At first he'd seemed to want me to catch him. Now I felt he was trying to lose me.

Yorkville is crisscrossed by lanes and alleys. The boy dodged down them. He couldn't fool me. I'd lived around that district all my life. I was hoping he'd try one alley too many and find himself in a dead end. No such luck.

He headed through the revolving doors of a mall, sending them spinning and gaining himself some time. Crutches aren't the easiest things to manoeuvre through revolving doors.

Once inside, I didn't know which route he'd taken. I headed for the courtyard. From there, through the windows, I could watch all four sides of the mall. He made for one of the exits. I took off after him.

As the afternoon daylight faded, the day got colder and in places the wet streets turned slick. Light from the street lamps turned people into black shadows. Their parcels became part of them, giving them grotesque shapes, even as they wandered across the sidewalk to ooh and aah at the window displays. There they stood like silhouettes, gazing into glass caves where dolls and nodding elves came to life, while Christmas lights twinkled in the nearby trees.

Nothing seemed real any more. It was like a dream. I tried to keep my eye on the boy, but his black hair and black leather jacket made him difficult to see against the gleaming sidewalks. I lengthened my stride and swung along in great kangaroo leaps. My crutches thumped on the sidewalk. Shadowy sightseers crossed in front of me. I tried to dodge around them. The angle was more than my crutches could take. One of them slipped. Next thing, I was spread-eagled on the sidewalk. After all that effort, I'd lost the witch boy.

A couple of passersby hauled me to my feet and handed me my crutches. Fighting back tears of frustration, I tried to thank them. I'd fallen in front of a small café and a waitress came out. She invited me inside to sit down for a while. Gratefully, I followed her.

The kind waitress brought me a cup of coffee, "courtesy of the management," and left me to recover. As I sipped I gradually stopped trembling. By the time I'd finished the coffee I was calm enough to thank the waitress and start back for Dad's shop.

On the way, I kept a sharp lookout for the boy. Several times I thought I glimpsed him, but he was up to his old tricks again. Now you see me, now you don't. Over and over I asked myself why he had led me on that wild goose chase. What was the point? If he wanted the box, why wouldn't he at least talk to me about it?

Luckily, when I got back to the shop Mrs. Menzies was busy with a customer, so I didn't have to make excuses. I slipped upstairs to the apartment to clean up.

The shop is on a corner and there are two

flights of stairs leading to the apartment: one from inside the shop and one from an outside door that opens onto the side street. As I got to the top of the shop stairs, I thought I heard the outside door click shut. I decided it was Dad back from the hospital, so I went to the top of the other flight to say hi.

There was no Dad. No anyone. Thinking I'd been hearing things, I went on my way to the bathroom. The drawers in the vanity were open. Dad had left in a hurry.

I sponged myself off. After that, I felt calmer, and went to the kitchen to make a snack for me and Mrs. Menzies. Now that the Christmas shopping had started, we didn't usually take time to go out for supper.

Some of the kitchen cupboard doors weren't shut. Dad, I thought, you'd better smarten up. Vivian sure wouldn't like this if she could see it. I peeked into the living-room to see how he'd been doing there. At first I thought the weekly cleaning lady had been careless about putting vases and ornaments back in their proper places. Vivian has her treasures artistically arranged. Now they were all lumped together. I started moving them back the way they usually were.

It was then that I noticed dust-free patches where things had been, and dust under where they now stood. Someone had moved them. Not Dad, or the cleaning lady. A stranger.

The same one who'd been in our house? My heart started to pound. I looked in some of the cupboards and drawers. I was sure things had been disturbed. Vivian is a very tidy person. There was no sign of the relic box.

The boy! But how could it have been him? He'd been too busy leading me on a wild goose chase to break into the apartment. He must have an accomplice. But how could anyone get in? When you have an apartment full of expensive antiques, you don't fool around with cheap locks. And Mrs. Menzies would have seen anyone who tried to come through the back of the shop. What if I'd only imagined I'd seen him out there on the streets? Maybe he really did have some power over me.

Somehow, I got my nerves under control and made sandwiches for me and Mrs. Menzies. I didn't want her to see that anything was bothering me. I saved that for when Dad came back from the hospital.

His face looked grey instead of its usual healthy colour. He said he didn't feel like eating. I hated to worry him but I had to tell him about the burglary. He went upstairs to have a look. When he came down he looked even more worried than before.

"There doesn't seem to be anything missing, Katy," he said. "Your imagination must be working overtime."

Maybe he was right. Maybe I was cracking up. Maybe this was part of the witch's curse — making me lose my mind. I wiped the sweat off my forehead and tried again.

"Dad!" I said. "Everything is so untidy."

"I'm turning into a slob."

That wasn't true. He was making excuses. I played my trump card. "What about the relic box?" I asked. "Where is it?"

"In the safe," Dad said. "Vivian wanted it put away."

"Please check the safe, Dad," I said. "See if the box is missing."

"Okay," he said, "if you really think I should."

He opened the safe. The relic box was still there, the cat on top smiling more smugly than ever. Defeated, I slumped down on the nearest chair.

First our house burgled, now Dad's apartment. I was sure there was a connection. Even Toronto can't have that many burglars — especially ones who don't take things.

Dad stood staring at me with an anxious expression. He looked as if he wanted to say something but didn't know exactly what.

Adam and Mother didn't believe in curses, or witches. I could accept that. Even Jenny had to come up with her mind theories. I blamed her shrink. But now it was Dad. I could see it in his eyes. He didn't believe in the witch boy, or the curse, or even that his apartment could have been burgled by an ordinary mortal. My own father thought I was out to lunch.

Nobody but me realized what was happening — nobody except Vivian — and she was stuck in the hospital unable to do anything. The witch had taken care of her.

I was on my own.

Chapter 10

Dad in Danger

The following Saturday I arrived at the shop shortly after nine-thirty, opening time. It was still shut. I hammered on the door. After a while Dad came through from the back to let me in. He was wearing a dark blue silk dressing gown that usually makes him look rich and famous. That morning, the dressing gown was askew and his hair was all over the place.

"Hi, Dad," I said. "What's wrong? As soon as I walked into the shop, I smelled smoke. You burned breakfast?"

"Not exactly." Embarrassed, Dad ran his fingers through his hair. "I fried some chicken for supper last night."

"You shouldn't eat fried foods," I scolded.

"I know. Serves me right," he admitted. "Anyway, while it was cooking I thought I'd lie down for a minute. The next thing I knew Sam landed with a thump on my chest and started raking me with his claws. I woke up, cursing Sam, to find the smoke detector screaming, the sprinklers showering me, and the kitchen full of smoke. Luckily, I was able to put out the fire on the stove with the extinguisher. Talk about chicken flambé!" Angrily, I turned on him. "It's not funny. You could've been killed. How come the smoke detector didn't wake you?"

"I was dreaming I was in the shower with the alarm ringing," he said. "I couldn't shut the wretched thing off."

"Since when d'you keep an alarm clock in the shower?" I asked. I couldn't help being mad at him for nearly getting himself killed.

"Since when do dreams have to make sense?" Dad said.

I headed for the stairs to see the damage.

"Don't go up there," Dad said. "The floors are still slick from the sprinklers. Your crutches might slip. And, Katy, you're not to mention this to Vivian. There's nothing she can do about it right now and I don't want her worrying. I'll have the whole mess cleaned up by the time she and the baby come home."

"How is Vivian?" I asked.

He shook his head. "Lying in hospital isn't good for her. There's nothing to take her mind off . . . off . . . her troubles." I knew what he meant. He left me to look after the shop while he went upstairs. Thee and thine shall suffer and perish. Gratefully, I hugged Sam who was sitting on his chair giving himself a good wash. "Clever cat," I said. "It's thanks to you Dad's still alive. But what are we going to do about Vivian and her baby?"

While Dad was upstairs, I phoned Mother. He'd said, "don't tell Vivian," not "don't tell your mother," and I had to tell someone.

It was Mother's day off. She and Adam had been planning to do some Christmas shopping, but I caught them before they left.

"Poor Bob," Mother said. "Adam and I will drop by later."

Mid-morning, I was helping a customer when I glanced through the window and saw a weird-looking trio peering into the shop window. Yorkville has its share of eccentrics, but I'd never seen these three before. The woman waved a mop at me. She looked angry. My stomach did a somersault. I was alone in the shop and I wasn't sure I could cope with anything unusual that morning. I took a quick second look.

It wasn't a weirdo, it was my own mother. She was wearing an old jogging outfit and her hair was wrapped in a scarf. In one hand she carried a pail. With the other, she brandished one of those mops with a shaggy, cotton head.

Adam loomed behind her. He had on his camel hair jacket and a skiing toque and he carried our "shop" vacuum — the kind that sucks up water as well as dirt. He looked like Paddington Bear on his way to clean up the ski slopes.

Jenny, wearing her oldest jacket and jeans, poked her head around the door. Of the three she was the most respectable, although the huge plastic bag full of old rags made her look a bit like a bag lady. "Psst," she hissed. "Come here."

I excused myself to the client and carefully wended my way to the shop door. Crutches are dangerous weapons in an antique store. I stared at my family.

"Open the side door," Jenny said. "We can't come through the shop like this."

"That's for sure," I said. "You just about scared me out of my wits."

"Don't be smart," Mother said. "Where's your father?"

"Gone to the bank."

"Good," Mother said. "I'm glad he's out of the way."

"We've come to clean up the apartment," Adam said. "It must be a mess. Your father's having more than his share of trouble lately."

Naturally! If he and Mother weren't so blinded by their own prejudice, they'd know why Dad was having trouble.

I let them in at the side door and they filed upstairs, their equipment clanking. Jenny came last. I tugged at her sleeve. "Dad could've been killed," I whispered.

"Forget it, Katy," she said. "He was tired. That's all."

"Sure," I said sceptically. "If only I hadn't lost that boy. I'm sure the box is his. I've just got to get it back to him. The problem is — how?"

"Okay," Jenny said. "Forget the cloak and dagger stuff. Do the obvious."

"Like what?" I asked.

"Put the box in the shop window, where he can't miss it. When he sees it he'll come for it, then you can nab him."

"What if an ordinary customer wants to buy the box?"

"Put a special sticker on it," Jenny said. "A red dot, or something, or a label saying DISPLAY ONLY. Then you can say it's on hold for someone. That's no lie."

Mother came to the top of the stairs. "Jenny," she called. "I thought you came along to help."

While I waited on customers, I could hear the vacuum humming overhead. When Dad came back he went straight upstairs. Later I heard the work party leaving by the side door.

When Dad came down he said, "It was good of your mother and Adam and Jenny to clean up for me like that."

"I would've helped too," I said. "But someone had to keep shop."

"I know, Katy," he said, and he kissed my forehead. "I really appreciate all you're doing."

His eyes got kind of watery. "One thing I'll say for adversity," he said, "it sure has a way of bringing families together." On his way upstairs, he grabbed a tissue and blew his nose loudly.

Christmas was only a week and a half away. Mrs. Menzies and I were doing a brisk business, but the only customer I wanted to see was the witch boy. Every time I remembered the fire, I felt sick. From time to time, I glanced at the window where I had placed the relic box front and centre.

After a while, a customer in wire-rimmed glasses came in. He was looking for a present for his wife, and couldn't make up his mind between two Victorian statuettes.

"Why not take them both?" I suggested. "They really are a pair." They were, too. All curls and dimples and flowing robes, making eyes at one another over marble columns.

While he was dithering, my attention was caught by a customer at the counter. She wore jeans and a short jacket with the hood up. Her back was to me.

Mrs. Menzies was behind the counter. "I'm sorry," she said. "This box is not for sale. It's on hold."

The customer wasn't taking no for an answer. I heard her arguing. She had a light, girlish voice. She'd taken the relic box out of the window. Probably she'd decided it would make a great gift for her mother. Wait till she heard the price! I was about to go and help Mrs. Menzies when there was a ruckus at the door.

It was Dad. Two men were supporting him. I knew them. Rosie and Fern, we called them. They owned the florist shop next door. Rosie had pink cheeks. Fern had a lot of wrinkles.

Dad's face was a nasty green colour and he was holding his stomach. I tipped Sam off his chair, and Rosie and Fern lowered Dad onto it.

"Call an ambulance," said Fern.

"Might be his heart," Rosie said.

"Don't be ridiculous," Dad said. "It's something I ate." He groaned. "I'll never eat at that filthy bistro again."

My customer put down the statuettes. "I'm a doctor," he said. "Maybe I can help." He asked Dad some questions, felt his pulse, peered into his eyes and made him stick out his tongue. "It could be your gall bladder," he said. "But you should go the hospital. It never pays to take chances."

"I've been poisoned," Dad said. Muttering vengeance on the bistro, he staggered to the back of the shop. Rosie volunteered to drive Dad to the hospital.

On her way home from a music lesson, Jenny decided to come by the shop to say hello to Sam. She arrived just as Fern and Rosie were loading Dad into Rosie's car. "I'll go to the hospital with Dad," she said, in her new, grown-up way.

I opened my mouth to argue. I wanted to go. This was the boy's second attempt to get Dad. Third time lucky. Isn't that what they say? I was frantic.

"Katy," Jenny said, before I could get a word out, "don't you have to help Mrs. Menzies? Besides, Dad can't very well lean on you when you're on crutches." As she swept off, she called over her shoulder, "Phone Mother and tell her what's happened. I think she'd like to know." She sounded as cool as a cucumber.

I phoned Mother. I meant to be cool too. The ice princess. As soon as I tried to talk, I broke down.

Mrs. Menzies talked to Mother. When she put the phone down, she said sympathetically, "Your mother says you're to wait here. Adam will pick you up."

Mrs. Menzies turned our Open sign to Closed and locked the shop door. "Oh, my goodness!" she said. "That little silver box. It's gone. I left it on the counter. Katy, did you put it away?"

I hadn't. We looked to see if maybe the young woman had put it back in the window. It wasn't there. We looked everywhere. No relic box.

"She took it," Mrs. Menzies said indignantly. "That customer. She stole it while we were busy with your father. I can't understand how anyone could behave that way."

Of course she couldn't understand. Mrs. Menzies knew nothing about the curse. It didn't surprise me. There's probably a law of curses that says, "If anything can go wrong, it will." Things would get worse, too. Now that the box had been stolen, there was no way we could give it back to the witch. We'd be cursed forever.

Adam came. "Your mother's gone to the hospital to see if there's anything she can do," he said.

"There's nothing she can do. It's his heart," I blubbered. "I'll probably never see him again."

Adam gathered me in his arms. He has broad shoulders and a wide chest. He doesn't smell chic the way Dad does. Most of the time he smells of wet wool. But Adam was made for crying on. Like an old teddybear.

He patted my back and I sensed that, in a funny kind of way, he was happy. Not happy because I was grief-stricken, but happy because he felt he was being a comfort to me — like a father. Adam wanted to be a father to Jenny and me. It wasn't his fault we already had one we loved with all our hearts.

"Katy," he said. "Katy, listen to me. Your father isn't having a heart attack. And he's not going to die. They think it's his gall bladder. They're keeping him in for tests. He'll be okay. Believe me."

Of course Adam would say that Dad would be okay. He doesn't believe in curses.

As far as Adam is concerned, everything has an explanation. No hidden demons. No evil forces. When Adam looks at a tree he sees a tree. He doesn't see evil chomping away at its leaves, or gnawing at its insides. To him, it's just caterpillars and wood beetles having their dinner.

"That's how life is, Katy," he says when I complain about the cruelty of nature. "Everything has to eat. Trees and insects don't worry the way we do."

The way Adam talks you'd think a caterpillar enjoys being someone's dinner. You can almost hear it clapping its dozens of little legs together when some beady-eyed bird swoops down on it.

In the room behind the shop there was a chesterfield waiting to be re-covered. Adam guided me to it. "I'm going upstairs for a minute," he said.

He came back with a pillow and a quilt. "There," he said. "You lie down. Put your leg up and rest."

"You don't understand," I said, between sobs. "We've lost the relic box."

Adam's face puckered in puzzlement.

"Yes," said Mrs. Menzies. "A customer stole it. It's a valuable piece. And it was on hold for a client."

"Don't worry," Adam said. "It'll be insured."

He didn't understand at all.

"You've had a hard time lately, what with your leg and everything," he said. "I'll help Mrs. Menzies clear up. You lie here and rest."

I don't think Vivian would've been too thrilled if she could have seen Adam tucking that quilt around me. It was the same one she took off the bed every night and draped on the quilt stand. It was antique, handmade, and worth several hundred dollars. Adam didn't notice. He didn't care about things like quilts. But he did care about me. He couldn't help it if he truly didn't believe in things like curses.

Adam and Mrs. Menzies finished clearing up. "Would you like to go to the hospital and see your dad?" Adam asked.

"Yes, please," I said.

When we got to Dad's room, Jenny was sitting beside his bed. Dad's eyes were closed.

"The doctor gave him something to make him sleep," Jenny whispered.

"Where's your mother?" Adam asked.

"She's gone to the maternity floor," Jenny said. "Someone had to tell Vivian. Mother thought she. . . ."

Adam nodded.

Mother came back pushing Vivian in a wheelchair.

"Oh, Bob!" Vivian said with a little moan.

Mother put her hand on Vivian's shoulder. "He'll be fine," she said. "Lot's of people have gall bladder operations. There's nothing to worry about."

I just about freaked out. "Are you crazy?" I wanted to scream. "What about that witch and his curse?"

Chapter 11
Running Out of Time

Our school holidays started. By then, I was so worried, it hardly even registered. Adam's holidays started, too. He and Jenny said they'd take turns helping Mrs. Menzies and me at the shop. Jenny didn't have a lot of time to spare. She was practicing for a Christmas piano concert. Mother still had to work at the library.

"I wish I didn't have to," she said. "I'd like to help."

"I thought you hated the shop," Jenny said.

Jenny and I were in the kitchen helping Mother make supper. I was peeling potatoes, Jenny was making the salad and Mother was whipping up something for dessert.

Mother stopped the mixer and stared into space. "I think my dislike of the shop had more to do with an unhappy marriage than it had to do with antiques," she admitted.

Absentmindedly, she began cleaning off the beaters with her finger. "Girls," she said, "I want you to know that, even though we're divorced, I still love your father." She sighed. "Oh dear, that didn't come out right, did it? What I mean is, I love him, but in a different way from the way I love Adam." She sucked the cream off her finger.

I couldn't believe my eyes. Ever since she and Dad got divorced, Mother has been very careful about her weight. She never eats dessert. That includes not tasting. Usually Jenny or I get to do that.

"Do you understand?" she asked.

Jenny said she understood. I said so, too. But I didn't. Not really. Later I took it up with Jenny.

"What kind of person do we have for a mother?" I said. "How can she still love Dad when she loves Adam?"

"Simple," Jenny said. "She loves Adam because he makes her happy. She loves Dad because he makes her miserable."

"Brilliant," I said. "Now it's all clear. Clear as mud."

"My shrink says that love and hate are two sides of the same coin," Jenny said. "When you love someone you think everything should be perfect. If the one you love behaves in a way you don't like, you hate him or her for disappointing you. That's why Mother and Dad got divorced.

Love and hate — two sides of the same coin."

"I still don't see how she can love two men at the same time," I said.

"Katy," Jenny said, "there's no limit to the number of people a person can love."

I didn't stop to think about what Jenny said. I had more important things on my mind. I'd been thinking — a lot — about the girl who stole the relic box. And the more I thought, the more convinced I'd become that she was the witch boy's sister. She was the right size. She'd sounded the right age. If only I'd seen her face.

Mrs. Menzies wasn't much help. "Just an ordinary girl," she said. "Nothing remarkable about her. I didn't see the colour of her hair. She kept her hood up."

Later in the week, Vivian phoned Mrs. Menzies and me at the shop. When it was my turn to talk, she said, "Mrs. Menzies says she doesn't know what she'd do without you."

I never know what to say when people pay me compliments. "Just say thank you," Jenny says. Somehow, that sounds to me as if you think you deserve the praise. "How's Dad?" I countered.

"Irritable," Vivian said. "He hates being sick. And he's impatient to get the operation over with. But the doctor wants him to feel better before they do it."

"That makes a lot of sense," I said. "The minute he feels better, operate. That way they make sure he won't feel better for long. Crazy doctors."

"Katy," Vivian said, "are you worried about your father?" If there was anyone who would understand, it was Vivian. Dad had told her about the relic box being stolen. "Sure I'm worried," I said. "Who wouldn't be?"

"But your father said you thought the girl who stole the box was the little boy's sister — the one you saw at the auction sale. In that case we don't have to worry any more. If the boy has his box back, he's happy and everything is back to normal, isn't it?" For the first time in weeks she sounded totally cheerful.

"I guess so," I agreed. I wasn't convinced, but I didn't want to upset Vivian when she was feeling better.

"So, you see, you don't have to worry about your father, Katy. He'll be fine."

I thought about what she'd said. If the witch boy had his beloved box back, he'd remove the curse. That made sense. Except, as far as I could see, he hadn't. Dad still had to have an operation. Vivian still had to stay in hospital. What was so great about that?

Things weren't going all that well for me, either. Six weeks had gone by, but the doctor decided I had to wear my cast for another two. I didn't so much mind having a fresh cast, it was the sight of my shrunken leg muscles that made me want to howl. I couldn't imagine how

I'd ever dance again.

Adam came to pick me up from the doctor's office and drive me home. He dropped me in front of our house and raced back to the shop.

Out on the sidewalk, I could hear Jenny playing the piano in our basement, practicing for her Christmas concert. She was playing a selection of Christmas music — carols and some other things — arranged in a medley. It wasn't the sort of carol music you could sing along to. The piano did the singing.

Our house is right downtown and although the people who live in our neighbourhood are very respectable, a fair number of not-so-respectable people use the street. Usually I don't look directly at them. It's safer that way.

That day, a small group had gathered outside our house. Two winos sat on cushions of newspaper, eyes closed, leaning against our front yard wall. Three young punks were draped around the tree at the edge of the sidewalk.

Mr. and Mrs. Chomsky from down the street stood arm in arm at the edge of the lamplight. The light caught Mr. Chomsky's white cane. Everyone was very still, as though the pool of light cast a pool of peace. But I knew it wasn't the light that was making them feel that way. It was Jenny's music.

As I opened the gate, she stopped playing.

One of the young punks detached himself

from the tree. "Hey," he said, "you know the guy playing that piano?"

I sensed he didn't mean any harm. "It's not a guy, it's my sister."

"Ask her to play again."

I knew why he wanted to hear Jenny play again and, suddenly, I knew why I wanted to dance. I wanted to do what Jenny did with her music. The applause I wanted wasn't for myself — well, not totally — the applause tells you you've done what you wanted to do. You've got through to people. You've touched their hearts, or their minds.

And I had to wait to find that out until I knew I might never dance again. "Thanks, witch boy," I said, bitterly. "Thanks for ruining my life."

Mother was busy writing Christmas cards when I came in. "Hello, Katy," she said, looking up. "Would you like a cup of tea? I was just going to have one." Mother and Adam drink herbal teas. They've declared war on caffeine.

I said I'd have the tea. I guessed why Mother offered it. She'd seen that I didn't look exactly bursting with happiness and it was her way of offering sympathy. Maybe she really did understand how depressed I felt about my leg. Even though she'd never come right out and say so.

After we'd agreed on Tangy Orange, she went to the kitchen to put the kettle on. I followed her.

"Vivian's going to have her baby tomorrow," she said.

"How d'you know?" I asked. "I thought he wasn't supposed to be born until Christmas Eve."

"The doctors think it's a good idea not to wait any longer," Mother said briskly.

So the boy had his box back and everything was great, was it? No way. Either there was something wrong with my theory and he didn't have his box, or he had the box, but he hadn't bothered to remove the curse. Whichever it was, I had to find him. And soon — before Dad had his operation and before Vivian had her baby. Time was running out.

Chapter 12

A Hunch

While I was out of the shop, someone had come in and bought Dora's painting.

"We should let Mrs. Hayley-Smith have the cheque," Mrs. Menzies said the next day. "I'm sure she'd like it before Christmas."

At first, Dora had come in every few days to see if the picture had sold, but she hadn't been in lately.

"I'll phone," I said.

Dora answered the phone. "Hello, Dora," I said (by that time I'd got used to calling her that), "this is Katy Martin. We've sold the picture and we have a cheque for twelve hundred dollars for Mrs. Hayley-Smith. Would you like to pick it up?"

"Oh!" She gave the shocked little gasp that I'd come to expect. "You've sold it?"

There was a pause, then she said, "Could you mail the cheque?"

"We could," I said, "but I don't think it would reach you before Christmas. There's so much mail at this time of year."

"Oh," she said. "Very well. I'll come in."

She sounded disappointed. But we'd got more for the picture than we'd promised. She should have been thrilled.

"Thank you," I said.

My tone might have been a little chilly. Anyway, Dora decided to be a bit more friendly.

"How are you, Katy, my dear?" she asked. "I suppose you have your cast off by now?"

"I have to wear it for another two weeks," I said. "I guess the doctors know best."

"Oh dear, I'm so sorry," she said. As usual she sounded totally sincere. "And how is your father?"

"He's still in the hospital," I said.

"How worrying," she said. "I do hope he'll soon be better." One thing you could say for Dora, she showed a lot of sympathy for people. "Please give him my best wishes. I . . . I'll come in for the cheque."

It wasn't until later that the light went on in my brain. How did Dora know that Dad was in hospital? "Stupid!" I told myself. "She was being polite, that's all. 'How's your father?' What's so unusual about someone asking that?" But Dora hadn't sounded surprised to hear that Dad was in the hospital, and she hadn't asked what was wrong with him.

Why not? Dora was the mouse who lived on crumbs from other people's lives. Dora was the kind of person who'd want to know all about someone's illness.

I was jumping to conclusions. But I couldn't shake my hunch. Dora knew the box had been stolen! She'd expected our whole family to be restored to health and happiness. That's why she'd sounded so upset when she'd heard we weren't.

For a while I wondered if Dora had come to the shop in disguise and stolen the box herself, but I'd have recognized her voice. No. The girl who had stolen the relic box was the sister of the witch boy and, somehow, they and Dora were connected. The question was — how?

When Jenny and Adam came to relieve Mrs. Menzies, I told them I was going out. "We sold Mrs. Hayley-Smith's picture," I said. "I'm going to take the cheque over. I could use a break from this place and Mrs. Menzies wants to do the bookkeeping. She'd like to get rid of the cheque."

My story was close enough to the truth to convince them, but what I really wanted was an excuse to see Dora again and do some snooping around Hayley Manor. I couldn't help feeling that if I really wanted to find the witch boy, Hayley Manor was the place to look.

Adam wanted to drive me, but I told him Jenny needed his help more than I did. He couldn't split himself in two, so he let me go. I almost wished he hadn't. Buses aren't designed for people with their legs in casts. I leaned against the window and put my leg up. I took up two seats, but it was the only way. It was a dreary December day, not exactly raining, but cold and damp. You'd have thought there was no such thing as a white Christmas. The windows fogged up so that I couldn't tell where I was. The bus jogged along, jolted to a stop to let people on and off, jogged and jolted, until I felt as if I'd travelled to the ends of the earth. Finally I asked the driver for the stop closest to Casa Loma. From there, even on crutches, I could walk the rest of the way.

Grey clouds hung low over the damp roofs. Along the sidewalk, the trees oozed water — slow, irregular drops fell from their leafless branches. Mansions, behind mossy stone walls, loomed out of the mist. I was the only one on the street. The thud of my rubber-tipped crutches on the sidewalk echoed dully, as though the ghost of Long John Silver were following me.

Eventually, I reached Hayley Manor. The gates were closed, but not locked. Faced by those iron gates I almost lost my nerve. I remembered my first visit, when Dad had talked about people who practiced black magic. Once I was in the grounds of Hayley Manor, hidden from the road by high walls, I could cry for help and no one would hear. I did a great job of spooking myself and, this time, it was no fun at all. Then I thought about the witch boy's curse and what it was doing to Dad and Vivian and me. I took a deep breath and pushed the gate open.

It swung smoothly. Someone, probably the major, had oiled it. There were no creaks. Quietly I closed it behind me and set off up the curving driveway as silently as I could. I wanted the element of surprise on my side.

And then I saw him. The witch boy.

He was peering at me from behind one of the huge trees beside the driveway. At first I thought he might be fooling me again. Was I really seeing him, or only his image?

The rock that hit me was hard and sharp. Real! No doubt about it. I felt it right through my jacket. The witch boy watched me, his eyes cold. He bent to pick up another rock. On crutches, there was no way I could use my arms to defend myself. I felt totally helpless. How had I ever imagined I could take on a witch? Then a second rock cut my forehead.

I never thought I'd be grateful for losing my temper. But when that second rock hit me, it made me so furious I hardly felt the pain. Witch or not, the boy had already hurt me enough. I wasn't going to take any more. At least, not without a fight. I lunged for him.

He grinned and dodged away through the trees. The grass was covered with patches of dirty snow and wet leaves. I slipped, recovered, and lurched after him. One crutch caught in some tree roots and I almost fell headlong.

How stupid could I get! We'd been through this before. He was leading me on. I couldn't catch him, so why try? Let him come to me. I pretended to trip again and crumpled into a heap. He stood a little way off and watched.

"Get up," he ordered. "Catch me."

"I can't," I said. "I'm hurt." I was surprised I could get the words out. My throat was tight with fear.

He ran over to me, and I reached out and caught his ankle. He fell and I rolled on top of him.

"Got you," I said, pinning his shoulders against the soggy ground.

"Let me go," he demanded.

As I looked down at him I almost obeyed. The image in the ballet studio mirror had come back to haunt me. In my imagination, I could see his face distorting — his bright eyes growing pale and misty, his full lips tight and thin, his smooth eyelids loose and reptilian, and the fine hair of his eyebrows grey and coarse. A wave of nausea swept over me. I was afraid I was going to faint.

Then I remembered a story I'd read somewhere. It was about a Greek hero who had to capture a monster. His helper goddess told him it would change into all kinds of horrible things, but he mustn't let it go. No matter what.

Hang on, I told myself. You can't give up now. Whatever happens, you've got to hang on. I squeezed my eyes shut so that I wouldn't have to watch.

The boy squirmed and wriggled and tried his best to get away. Normally he might have been able to, because I'm not very big for my age, but normally I don't wear a cast that weighs half a tonne. I kept him pinned down. He struggled harder.

"Let me go," he yelled. "Clare! Help!"

Maybe he was summoning an assistant. I remembered his sister and my heart sank. Now I'd have to face two of them.

No one answered. The wet trees deadened his cries.

I got up enough courage to take a quick peek at him. He hadn't changed. He stopped fighting and began to cry.

For a minute I almost felt sorry for him and let him up. Then I felt blood trickling from the gash on my forehead into my eyes. Maybe his tears were just another trick. Still holding him down with one hand, I wiped the blood away with a quick swipe.

"Let me up," he begged. "Please."

I couldn't understand it. What had happened to his supernatural powers? But now was no time to give up my advantage. "No way," I said. "Not until you remove your wretched curse."

His tears stopped and he smiled shrewdly. "You'd better be careful," he warned. "I know lots of spells. I put them on people."

"I know," I said. "You're a witch. You put your curse on the relic box. Why? What has anyone in my family ever done to hurt you?"

"You took my magic box that Grandfather gave me."

"And now you've got it back again," I said.

"No, I haven't."

"Don't lie to me," I said, pushing harder on his shoulders. "Your sister stole it."

He winced, then his eyes narrowed, sizing me up. "How do you know?"

I was playing a hunch, but I wasn't about to admit it. "I know your sister stole the box," I said. "And I know who broke into our house and into my father's apartment. I haven't told the police yet, but I can."

He seemed impressed. "Are you a witch, too?" he asked. His question surprised me. It sounded so innocently childlike. And I still couldn't figure out why he didn't change again, or at least slip out of my grasp. There must be some limits to his powers. Otherwise, he wouldn't mistake me for a witch. Maybe I could fool him.

The clouds pressed close, as if their weight would break the black, gnarled branches that twisted over our heads.

Everything was still — the way it is before a snowstorm —waiting. The day was on my side. It was worth a try.

I let my long, limp hair fall forward as I leaned over him. I put my bruised and bloodied face close to his. "I have supernatural powers," I said. "But a person does not become a witch overnight. A person must study. And when I become a witch I shall work for good, not for evil as you do."

He smiled in his sardonic way. "I don't have to study. I was born a witch." Coldly curious, like a child dissecting a fly, he asked, "Do you hate me?"

"No," I said. "I feel sorry for you."

He looked indignant. "Why?"

"Because hate destroys. It is destroying you." I made my voice low and menacing. "Hate drains the energy out of you, little by little. It leaves you empty and dry. A husssk. Like an inssssect that's been ssssucked dry by a ssspider."

He began to snivel. "It's not my fault. I can't help being bad. My mummy and daddy died. They shouldn't have left me. Aunt Mag took my magic box. Grandfather gave it to me. He said I should have it. He said I should've been his child. He said I was like him, different from other people. I wish my grandfather was here."

Aunt Mag! So that was the connection. I'd always suspected that Mrs. Hayley-Smith was a liar, but I'd never thought she'd go that far. My mind was reeling.

It didn't help that her nephew the witch boy sounded a lot like a mixed-up kid, and not very much like a witch. "Such an unhappy child," Vivian had said.

"What's your problem?" I asked. "You've got your grandfather's box back again."

"No I haven't. If I had Grandfather's box, maybe I could bring my mummy and daddy back," he said wistfully.

Then he turned petulant again. "I've tried, but the spells don't work. I've got to get my box back. Aunt Mag took it. She never wants me to have it. She hates me. That's why I hate her. I hate everybody."

The more he talked, the less like a witch he sounded. How could I have been so wrong about him?

Something new occurred to him and he scowled suspiciously. "How come you don't know that Aunt Mag took my magic box?" he asked. "You said you were a witch."

I told you, I'm only a student witch," I said solemnly, the way I thought a witch might speak. "Now, tell me, child, what is your name?"

"Simon."

"Very well, Simon, let us go to the house together and I shall confront your misguided aunt. I will get your magic box back for you. I promise."

Chapter 13

Unhappy Kid

As soon as I let Simon up, he ran for the house. I followed him to the back door and knocked. His sister opened the door.

Behind her was what looked like a family room.

Simon's sister stared at me as if she'd seen a ghost. No wonder! I bet I was quite a sight — on crutches, with my leg in a cast, a gash on my forehead, blood smeared across my face, and bruises that had faded to a greenish yellow.

"Please, c-come in," she stammered. "Are you badly hurt?"

She didn't have to ask me who I was. She knew. "Simon," she said softly, "fetch a bowl of warm water and a clean cloth." Then trying, not very successfully, to look stern, she said to me, "What do you want?"

"It's no good pretending, Clare," Simon said. "She knows what you did. She's a witch. She knows you stole the magic box."

Clare turned pale. "I had to do it," she said. "We tried to get the box back at the auction sale, but your stepmother outbid Uncle Clive."

"Uncle Clive?"

"Major Hayley-Smith," Clare said. "Our uncle. He wanted to help us so he came to the auction in disguise. You see, Aunt Mag didn't want us to have the box, so we had to go behind her back. She thought she could get rid of the curse by selling the box."

I'd guessed as much.

"And then, when we'd finally got enough money together to buy it from your father, the clerk refused to sell it to me. And when I saw your father looking so ill . . . well, it seemed best to steal it while no one was looking. I was only trying to help. You do understand, Katy, don't you?" She sounded as though she might burst into tears.

I nodded. To be honest, I was having a hard time believing that this gentle, shy-looking girl would have the courage to steal anything. "And earlier you broke into our house to look for the box?"

Simon had come back with the water and first-aid supplies. He answered for her. "Don't be stupid. That wasn't Clare. That was Aunt Mag."

"Aunt Mag!" I had a mental picture of the large Mrs. Hayley-Smith, in her cotton dress and straw hat. "You mean Mrs. Hayley-Smith climbed the tree in front of our house and squeezed through Jenny's bedroom window?" I giggled helplessly. Clare looked anxious — as if she thought I was having hysterics.

"Goodness, no," she said. "Aunt Mag used the back door key that you keep in the milk chute. It was very easy." Right again!

"But why try to steal the box?" I asked. "I thought she wanted to get rid of it."

"When Aunt Mag heard that your stepmother might lose her baby, she felt terribly guilty," Clare said. "She realized the curse was working on your family. That didn't seem fair, so she tried to get the box back."

"But why steal it? Why not buy it? She's got lots of other things to sell."

Clare sighed. "Poor Aunt Mag. She felt terrible about having to sell our ancestral home in England. You see, it's been in the family for generations. She felt she'd let Simon and me down, particularly Simon. After our parents and older brother died in a car accident, Simon became the heir to the title. So now Aunt Mag thinks it's her duty to pass on the heirlooms she managed to keep. She thought if she stole the relic box from your father, he could collect the insurance and nobody would be out of pocket."

"Except the insurance company," I said. "Your aunt seems to have a rather hazy idea of right and wrong."

Clare blushed. "Try not to be too hard on her, Katy. Aunt Mag is a little eccentric, but she means well. She finally decided to sell the hunting picture so she could afford to buy the box, but before you could sell the picture, I stole the box."

"And the apartment over the shop?" I asked. "Who pulled off that little job?"

"Aunt Mag, of course," said Simon. "She was sorry about your leg, so she promised to get my box back if I helped her. So I made you chase me." He grinned. "It was fun, wasn't it?"

"Not specially," I said.

"Anyway, Aunt Mag couldn't find the box." He scowled. "How come you're asking so many questions? I thought you knew all about everything. You promised you'd get my magic box back for me."

"Okay," I said to Clare, trying to sound tough. "Where's the relic box now? Why haven't you given it back to Simon?"

She sighed. "Aunt Mag took it. She won't let Simon have it any more."

The room began to spin. Maybe it was from the blow to my head. More likely it was because I was so confused.

"You'd better lie down," Clare said anxiously. "You look a bit groggy. Simon, bring Katy a glass of water."

"Who put the curse on the box, anyway?" I asked.

"Our grandfather," Clare said. She gently washed the gash on my forehead and put a piece of clean gauze and some sticking plaster over it. While she was fussing, the door opened. There stood Dora with Major Hayley-Smith behind her. They stared at me as if I were a ghost.

"Oh!" Dora gasped. "Katy! What are you doing here?"

I struggled to a sitting position. It's hard to be sarcastic when you're flat on your back.

"I brought over the cheque for the picture," I said. "And guess what? I met your beloved Mrs. Hayley-Smith's nephew, Simon. And Simon says the relic box is his. His grandfather gave it to him. Only he says his Aunt Mag won't let him have it. And that it was Simon's grandfather, Mrs. Hayley-Smith's father, who put the curse on the box. How come your beloved Mag didn't tell my dad all this? How come you didn't? How come you both lied to us, Dora?"

"Dora!" Clare said, looking puzzled. "That's not Dora, that's Aunt Mag."

Chapter 14

The Rightful Owner

Dora collapsed into an armchair. The major cleared his throat several times and went to stand with his back to the woodstove.

"Aunt Mag!" Bug-eyed, I stared at Dora.

"It's true," she admitted. "I'm not Dora. I'm Mag — Mrs. Hayley-Smith. When your father said he wanted to talk to me about the relic box, I was afraid I might not be able to hide the truth from him. I persuaded my cleaning lady, Dora, to change places with me. For her it was like acting, not lying."

"Why did you have to lie?"

Shamefaced, she said, "I didn't want the relic box and its curse in the family. I thought if someone had bought the box, it would properly belong to the buyer and the curse wouldn't work on him or her."

"Evidently you were wrong," I said grimly. "My father has to have an operation, and my stepmother is going to have her baby before it's really due and I might never be able to dance again. So please give the relic box to Simon so that the curse can be lifted."

Dora (I still couldn't think of her as Mag) jumped out of her chair and paced up and down, wringing her hands.

"No," she cried. "I can't. I'm sorry, Katy, but I can't let Simon have it. It's a bad influence on him. The curse was my father's doing. He engraved the runes. He treasured that horrid little box. He used it to make . . . unpleasant . . . things happen to people."

"Only when they deserved it," Simon cried. "I found Grandfather's books, Katy. I told you. They tell how to put spells on people when they're mean to you. Grandfather used to put things in the magic box — things like dead toads and bits of plants. Then he'd get something from the person he wanted to put a spell on — nail clippings, or a bit of hair, or something. I read all about it."

"Take my advice, Simon," I said. "Find something else to read. That stuff's not suitable for a kid. You don't need it." Simon paid no attention. His eyes glowed with excitement. "Grandfather would hold the box between his hands, like this." He held his hands one above the other at chest level. "Then he'd close his eyes, say the magic words and make a spell." Simon began to mutter words that made no sense to me.

"Simon, please don't," cried Clare.

"Why?" Simon asked indignantly. "Nothing's going to happen. I'm not holding the magic box."

Dora had been scuttling back and forth like an agitated mouse. Now, her face white, her lips set in a determined line, she stopped in front of me. "You see! I won't let him have that wicked little box."

I was getting desperate. There I was on crutches, all alone in a house full of weird people, and feeling weak and wobbly. Not what anyone would call a position of strength to bargain from. I racked my brain for a solution — pretty tough when you're suffering from a blow to the head.

While I was thinking, the telephone rang. It was for me. "Katy, what's taking you so long?" Mother sounded angry, a sure sign she was worried. "Look, the doctors bungled things. They've scheduled it so that Vivian is having her baby and your father is having his operation at the same time. Adam and I are going to the hospital to hold their hands — Vivian's and your father's hands, I mean, not the doctors'. And I don't want you messing about on buses anymore today. Take a cab. We'll meet you at the hospital."

This was it. If I didn't hurry and get that curse removed, it would be too late. As I put the phone down, a numbing calm spread over me, rather like the way my face had turned numb after Nigel bashed it. That time, a horrible vision had appeared before me. This time, after I had quietly told Dora and the others what Mother had said, a possible solution began to emerge out of the calm.

"What if we tried this?" I said slowly. I felt excited and cautious all at the same time, almost afraid to believe this might be the way out. "If you don't want Simon to have the relic box, why don't you give it back to his grandfather?"

There was a small silence. Then the major suddenly came to life, cleared his throat and said, "Quite. Splendid solution."

"But, Katy, I told you," cried Clare. "Grandfather's dead."

"Maybe that doesn't matter," I said. "Maybe if we bury the thing, bury it with its rightful owner, we'll get rid of it forever."

"Oh, Katy," said Dora, with her usual little gasp. "That's a wonderful idea. But would it work, do you think? I mean if my father gave Simon the relic box, then Simon's the rightful owner, isn't he? Nothing can alter that."

"Maybe not," I said. "But Simon could lift the curse before giving the box back to his grandfather. And if Simon gives it back, it wouldn't be like anyone is keeping the box from him. We'd all be safe."

"I don't want to give the box back," Simon

pouted. "Everybody's mean to me. I need protection!"

"Forget it, Simon," I said. "Nobody's mean to you."

"Aunt Mag is," he muttered. "She hates me."

"Simon!" cried Dora, horrified. "That's not true. I love you. That's why I don't want you to have the relic box. I don't want you to turn into the kind of unhappy, revengeful man my father was."

"Then why won't you let me live with you and Uncle Clive?" Simon cried, scowling. "Why d'you send us away to boarding school? I hate it there. And I'm lonesome for Clare. Why can't we live here and go to ordinary schools?"

"Ordinary schools!" said Dora, horrified. "Oh no. No one in our family has ever done that."

I couldn't help butting in. "Listen, Dora," I said, "an ordinary school won't hurt Simon. Loneliness and unhappiness will. He needs to live with a loving family." Quite a speech. Jenny would have been proud of me. But I was desperate to get her to go along with my idea.

Dora sighed. "I can't bring his parents back. I wish I could."

Dora could take first prize in a nitwit contest. "Families don't have to be a mother, father and two kids," I said. "Look at our bizarre set-up. It works for us. We're a family." I hadn't thought of it that way before, but suddenly I could see it was true.

Dora gave me a long, thoughtful look before she said, "Simon, would you really be happier living here with Uncle Clive and me?"

"Yes, please, Aunt Mag. And Clare too," Simon said, sounding like a normal kid. Then he added shrewdly, "I think it's safer, don't you? If I get unhappy again, I don't know what might happen."

"First will you promise to remove the curse and bury the relic box?" I asked.

I never thought he'd go for it. I mean, that box really did give him a lot of power, or at least he thought it did. Maybe he wasn't such a brat after all. I was wishing Dora had made it clearer that her offer stood only if Simon gave back the box. But I needn't have worried. Simon saw his opportunity to do some bargaining. "Can I go into the crypt myself and give Grandfather the magic box, Aunt Mag?" he asked.

"I . . . I suppose so," Dora agreed, turning pale.

"And you won't send me or Clare to boarding school ever again?" he said.

"I promise I won't, Simon. I didn't know it meant so much to you."

Eyes shining, Simon turned to me. "The crypt is really neat, Katy. Really spooky. There are places in the wall for our ancestors' remains."

This kid was a real ghoul. Worse than Dee-Dee.

While I'd been arguing with Dora and Simon, Clare had slipped away. When she came back she was carrying the relic box.

Red-faced, she said, "I'm sorry, Aunt Mag, but I had to take this from your room. I don't think we should waste any more time — because of Katy's father and stepmother." Looking determined, she hooked her hair behind her ears and handed me the relic box. "Katy, take it and give it to Simon. Be quick and go with him to the crypt."

My stomach turned over. "Where is it?" I asked. I wasn't too eager to visit a graveyard after dark.

Clare was already putting on her jacket. "It's right here in the grounds," she said. "I'll bring a flashlight and go with you."

"Here's the key," said the major, removing a long key from a key-ring attached to his pocket. "Take it, Clare."

These people buried their relatives in their own backyard. My skin prickled as every hair on my body stood on end.

Neither the major nor Dora, I mean Mag, seemed at all anxious to visit the crypt. Their faces had a nervous, strained look. So did Clare's. But not Simon's. He could hardly wait long enough to put on a jacket.

The snowstorm that had threatened earlier had started. The air was full of big, soft flakes that deadened all sound.

Outside the grounds of Hayley Manor, the world seemed to have come to a standstill. Simon ran ahead.

"I don't need a light," he called out. "I can see in the dark."

With Clare holding the flashlight, we followed. We crossed a lawn edged with flower beds, then went down a gravel path between bare bushes.

"Be careful, Katy," Clare said. "At the end of the path there's a flight of steps. The ground falls away sharply. Beyond the steps the grounds have been allowed to go wild."

Once down the steps, we turned to the right. The lawn was above us at the top of a rocky wall. Simon, cradling the relic box, impatiently led the way along the side of the wall at the bottom. On crutches, I had to pick my way carefully. There was no moon and I could see only a few metres ahead where the pool of light from the flashlight bounced. I clung to that pool of light like a drowning man clings to a life preserver. If Clare should decide to switch it off . . . or the batteries died . . . I'd be left helpless in the dark.

"Here we are," Simon announced, stopping.

At first I couldn't see where we were. A black wall of rocks loomed on my right. A black wall of trees loomed on my left. Clare shone the beam of light on the rocks. There, like the entrance to a cave, was a hole in the wall. A short distance away, she lit up a second hole. Iron grilles covered both. "Back when the house was first built, the owner had this constructed," Clare said, sounding a bit embarrassed. "It's supposed to be an ancient ruin like the ones you see in Britain. Anyway, Aunt Mag decided it was the nearest thing to our family crypt that she was likely to find in Canada. After she sold our estate in England, she brought the ashes of my grandparents and my parents and brother here."

"Come on, Katy," Simon said, hovering at one of the cave entrances. "Hurry up. Don't you want to give Grandfather his box?"

Clare unlocked one of the grilles and opened it just enough for me to get through. "Can you handle the flashlight, Katy?" she asked timidly. "I'd rather not come inside, if you don't mind."

I took the flashlight and, somewhat reluctantly, followed Simon. Immediately, the fusty smell of damp air filled my nostrils. Simon went ahead. I hesitated. I couldn't help thinking of those iron grilles. Simon could easily knock my crutches out from under me and rush out, leaving me inside. I wished Clare had come with us. She had the key.

"Come on, Katy," Simon called.

I reminded myself that Mother and Adam knew I was at Hayley Manor. They'd know where to start looking if. . . . Somehow it didn't help much. Nervously, I followed Simon.

The cave had been bored into the rocky ground in a horseshoe shape. That accounted for the two entrances. In places it was barely high enough for me to stand upright and I had to bend my head as I lifted myself along on my crutches. We were a few metres inside when Simon stopped.

"Shine your light on the wall, Katy," he said. "This is where my parents' and brother's ashes are kept."

In the light of the flashlight, I saw a small cavity, lined with stones. Inside it stood an urn. Beside the urn was a photograph of a youngish man and woman in wedding clothes. Beside them was the photo of a teenaged boy wearing a school uniform. The pictures were faded and rippled by the damp. A bunch of dead flowers lay beside them.

"Those are my photos of my parents and brother," Simon said. "In the summer, whenever Aunt Mag will let me come, I bring them flowers."

He sounded so wistful that, in spite of my nervousness, my heart went out to him.

We went deeper into the cave. At the deepest point, Simon stopped again. This time, he put the relic box on the ground at his feet and made me move the light around until he found the special rock he was looking for. "See," he said, "this one's loose." He wriggled it until it came away. Then he stood on tiptoe and, with both hands, reached inside a hole. "Hold the light steady," he said. "You're moving it."

My hand was shaking.

"Got it," he said. With some difficulty, he pulled out of the hole a heavy, rectangular container. "It's made of really strong steel. I think Aunt Mag's scared that Grandfather might get out."

The cave was cold and clammy and smelled of wet earth. My head brushed against the stones. I couldn't shake the thought that I was in a grave, in danger of being buried alive. I wanted to scream at Simon to hurry.

Carefully, he set the container beside the relic box and opened it. Carefully, I avoided looking inside. Simon pulled out a small picture in a silver frame. "This is my picture of Grandfather," he said. "D'you want to see it?" He grabbed the flashlight from me and held it below the picture.

I almost lost my balance. Lit by the spotlight was a face I recognized. The face I'd seen in the studio mirrors on the day of my accident. The same hooded eyes and thin, downturned mouth. Speechless, I gaped at the picture. Simon didn't seem to notice my reaction. He put the picture back into the container. "Now," he said, with a satisfied sigh. "We're ready. You hold the light, Katy."

While I struggled to hold the flashlight steady, he took the relic box between his hands at chest level, as I'd seen him pretend to do in the house. His bright eyes intense, he gazed at me.

"As the rightful owner of this box, I do solemnly declare that, from this time forward, the curse on Katy's stepmother, and all her kith and kin, is lifted. Henceforward, let them be healthy and happy."

After he spoke we were both silent. I couldn't thank him for keeping his promise. My tongue was stuck to the roof of my mouth. I couldn't even move. My crutches dug into my armpits because I was leaning too heavily on them.

Simon crouched on his heels and held the relic box over the container at his feet. "And now, Grandfather," he said, "I return this box, which you so generously gave me, to your safekeeping." Gently he lowered the little relic box into the container and replaced the lid.

"There, Katy," he said. "I hope you're satisfied."

Satisfied with what he had done? Yes, I was. There was only one question left — would it work?

Chapter 15

How it Ended

Mother, Adam, Jenny and I looked at the baby through the window of the hospital nursery. Space-age nursery! Babies laid out in rows in plastic trays. Mother said it was to fight germs. There was a see-through cover over Vivian's baby's crib. He looked like Snow White in her glass coffin waiting for the loving prince to kiss her awake. But because he was a boy, it would have to be a princess.

"He's so small," I said.

Mother put her arm around my shoulders. "You weren't much bigger than that when you were born, Katy," she said, "and look at you now."

"Elephant," Jenny said. Her voice sounded kind of husky.

"Mighty oaks from tiny acorns grow," Adam quoted. "One of your everyday miracles." Then he sneezed three times. His eyes were red and watery.

"I hope you're not getting a cold," Mother said, as if he'd get a cold on purpose.

Adam grinned. "Just an allergy," he said.

On the way to Vivian's room, Mother checked at the nursing station. Dad was back from the operating room. Adam collected a wheelchair so that we could take Vivian to see him.

We all gathered around the bed and waited for Dad to wake up. When he opened his eyes, the first person he saw was Adam standing, red-eyed, at the foot of the bed, with Mother beside him.

"What's this?" he asked. "Awake? I feel lousy, but I'm not dead yet." He sounded quite angry. "If I hear any harp music, or catch sight of any winged people, I'll let you know."

"He's going to be fine," Mother said. "His temper's back to normal."

Then Dad saw Vivian sitting beside him. "The baby. Vivian, he's all right, isn't he?"

Vivian nodded. "I think so. He's very small."

"Don't worry, Dad," I interrupted, "I found the boy from the auction. His name's Simon. I gave him the relic box and he removed the curse. Everything's going to be great."

Dad gave a contented little sigh and smiled. "You mean you finally got rid of that Pandora's box? Well done, Katy. I always knew you were a smart girl." He closed his eyes. "Jenny, don't you have a piano recital tomorrow evening? I'm sorry

I can't be there. You know, the strangest thing happened. I dreamed I heard you playing, and very beautiful it was, too. For a minute I thought I had died and gone to heaven."

"Not you," Mother said. "Only the good die young."

"Thanks, Pam," he said. "That's very reassuring."

"He sounds fine to me," Adam said. "Maybe he and I should trade places."

Dad opened his eyes. "You do look sick, Adam," he said. "Why don't you go home and get a good night's rest? I'm tired. This station is closing down for the night." He closed his eyes again.

"Good night, sleep tight," Jenny said.

"Watch the bugs don't bite," I added.

He always used to say that to us when we were little.

"Vivian, would you like us to wheel you back to your room?" Mother asked.

Vivian shook her head. "No, thank you. The chair's quite easy to manage." She smiled at Mother. "Why don't you take Sneezy home? I'll stay with Grumpy for a while."

Mother grinned.

Vivian looked shyly at Mother and Adam, Jenny and me.

"You've all been so kind," she said. "Katy's been such a help in the shop, in spite of her crutches, and Bob told me how the three of you went to the apartment and helped him clean up after the fire."

Mother's like me. She finds it difficult to accept compliments. She shrugged. "What are friends for?" she said.

"You're more than friends," said Vivian. "You're family."

The next day we went to the hospital again. Dad was with Vivian. After a while the nurse came in with masks and white coats for us all to wear. "The baby's doing better than we expected," she said. "We thought he should visit with his family for awhile." Then she went and fetched the baby.

Vivian held him and we all tried to see what he looked like. It was tough when he was wrapped up like an Egyptian mummy.

"What's his name?" Jenny asked.

"Charles Robert," Vivian answered proudly.

"Very dignified," said Adam.

"Too dignified for a baby," Jenny said. "Can we call him Charley?"

Dad chuckled. "That's what his mother and I intend to call him."

"What colour are his eyes?" I asked.

"I don't know," Vivian said. "I've never seen him with his eyes open." She looked at me as if she wasn't sure how I'd react. "Katy, would you like to hold him?"

I felt kind of shy and awkward. I'd never held a newborn baby before. But I didn't want to insult his parents, so I sat down beside her on the bed and she laid Charley in my arms. He didn't exactly smell of talcum powder. He wasn't even soft and cuddly — mainly because of the tight blanket. He was just very small, very pink and very helpless-looking.

Suddenly I got a funny feeling; different from anything I've ever felt before. I couldn't help myself. I slipped my mask down, bent over and kissed his forehead. Charley opened his eyes. They were blue.

At that moment I totally lost my heart to a baby. Not only that, I felt overcome with love for everybody in the room. My entire family! I remembered what Jenny had said — "There's no limit to the number of people a person can love."

Jenny was right. I'd never have to worry about not having enough love for all of us. There was even some to spare. I felt wonderful.

"My turn," Jenny said. "Hand him over."

The next day was Christmas Eve. Mother had last-minute things to do. Adam, Jenny and I manned the shop so that Mrs. Menzies could have the day off. We closed at noon.

Jenny looked at Sam. "Poor Sam," she said. "I hate to leave him. He's going to have to spend Christmas alone."

Adam sighed. "What the heck! I couldn't be

more red-eyed and wheezy than I am already. Let's take him home for Christmas."

Now that's what I call love.

"Adam, you're a doll," Jenny cried. She threw her arms around his neck and kissed him. Adam went off whistling to buy a Christmas tree.

Jenny and I stayed behind to clear up. "You know, I still can't believe I could be so wrong about Dora," I admitted.

"Imagine her turning out to be Mrs. Hayley-Smith, and breaking into our house and the apartment. Some nerve! Some scared dormouse!"

"More like a cool cat," agreed Jenny. "And how about your little witch boy? I warned you not to let your imagination run away with you, didn't I?"

"Well, he may not be a witch," I said, blushing, "but even you have to admit there were a lot of funny things going on."

"Like what?" said Jenny.

"Like when Simon picked up the box at the auction and made the guy drop the vase."

"Coincidence," said Jenny serenely.

"Maybe. But Simon sure thinks the box has powers. And so do the Hayley-Smiths."

"Old family superstitions," sniffed Jenny. "Besides, if you'd had Simon's grandfather for a father, or a grandfather, or even a father-in-law, you'd believe in it, too. He sounds like a pretty scary guy."

"You can say that again," I said. "But there are other things I still don't understand. Like when I looked in the studio mirrors and saw Simon change into an old man . . ."

"Think about it, Katy. You were overwrought. You were in a lot of pain. You might even have had a concussion and passed out. My shrink says people often imagine things when they get a blow on the head."

I thought about it. "Well," I said at last, "I guess that could have been it...I'd just bashed my nose before I wrecked my leg. I should've quit while I was ahead. But there's something I still don't understand. How come the the old man I imagined looked exactly like Simon's grandfather? How could I possibly know, before I'd seen his picture, what he looked like? Ask your shrink to explain that."

"She can't," Jenny admitted. "I already asked her. But she's working on it. By the way, she'd like to meet you. She thinks you might be able to help her with some research she's doing."

"Forget it," I said. "I'm not running mazes for anybody."

"Anyway, I'm glad that curse business is all behind you and you're back to normal," Jenny said. "Normal for you, that is."

"You really think it was all in my mind, don't you? You think I even imagined seeing Simon when he wasn't there."

"Of course. Though, as my shrink says, it seemed real to you. She thinks you were upset by Vivian's pregnancy. She says you were probably afraid Dad wouldn't love you any more once he got Charley. It was all subconscious of course, but it kind of threw your mind into a spin."

To me, that sounded almost as far-fetched as believing in spells and warlocks. But I know now I got carried away, especially about Simon.

That scares me a bit. I mean, I don't like to think I have anything in common with those awful people who burned witches at the stake. They usually did it out of fear. In those days they had lots to be afraid of. And I know I got pretty scared when things were going wrong. But it doesn't do any harm to find out more about yourself. Remember what I said earlier? That people are like icebergs? Well, underneath the tip of my iceberg — the modern, scientific part — I discovered a part that still believes in magic. I'm not like Jenny or Mother or Adam, or even Dad. I don't decide that things are impossible, just because they aren't very likely. I guess that's okay. As long as I don't let it get out of hand. I intend to keep an open mind about what happened. Life is a lot more interesting that way.

The best Christmas gift I got was from Mother and Adam. They said they'd been making enquiries and they'd found a doctor who specialized in sports injuries.

"He's done some fantastic things for hockey players," Mother said.

"We've made you an appointment for the first week in January," said Adam.

The first week in January couldn't come fast enough. The sports injuries doc said he couldn't promise anything but he was almost sure I'd able to dance again, provided I was prepared to work really hard at my exercises. This is one thing no one will have to nag me about, ever. Besides, I'm getting some expert assistance.

Jenny's offered to help me develop my imaging techniques. And Simon says he's working on being a good witch now and he'll cast a few good spells to help me along. I didn't tell him not to. I figure it's all part of keeping an open mind.

Wish me luck.